DRAGON'S GODDESS

by

DEBRA ELISE

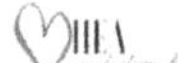

CONTENTS

ABOUT

Being kidnapped on the most important day of her career was not on Dr Britt Harmony's bingo card. Neither was discovering that the fairytales her late father spun were true.

A goddess-witch.

A shape shifting prince of the highlands.

Gods and monsters.

All of it.

True.

What she'd spent her life denying, and masking from others, has become a reality. And try as she might, she's unable to escape the handsome highlander who sets her body on fire.

If you knew your destiny would send you on the adventure of a lifetime but one misstep would either land you in the arms of a Duke of Hell or in the talons of a dragon shifter who claims he's your fated mate would you ever set foot in Scotland?

Does she even have a choice?

In Quinn Smythe's millennia long life, he never allowed himself to believe that the prophecy he and his brothers were saddled with by The Fates was real. After all, his parents had a flare for drama and control.

But when their Goddess mother, who has never respected boundaries, pops in at the absolute wrong time, and their absent otherworld sire decides it's time to reconnect in the middle of a battle with the demon threatening not only Britt but all of their mates in his quest to take over mankind, will Quinn and his brethren accept their mates and fulfill their destiny?

ACKNOWLEDGMENTS

I'd like to take this opportunity to say thank you to my editor, Karla with Oopsie Daisy Edits. She not only did an awesome job but she saved me from the dreaded … ellipsis monster!

My forever gratitude to the talented Anna-Lena Spies from Atra Luna Designs for the amazing cover. Thank you Anna!

And a special thank you to two of my beta readers for their continued support of my stories: Lynn Sell and Emily McCabe.

As always, a big thank you to my family for their love and support, Brian, Ian, Andrew, and Nancy and Ed Goodwin.

ONE

"Don't move. Don't scream...act as if you know me, and all will be well."

So engrossed in her thoughts, Britt heard the words, yet it took a moment for their warning to sink in. Certain she'd heard wrong; she looked up to see a man striding toward her. Yes, he was huge and imposing, but he was grinning. No, wait, maybe it was more of a grimace.

Dismissing him as a threat, she shook her head to rid the momentary sense of foreboding. He was probably having a conversation with someone using Bluetooth earbuds. And yeah, he was good-looking, but now wasn't the time for a flirtation.

On her way to give an important speech, perhaps the most important of her career, Britt Harmony couldn't afford to be waylaid. She nodded, then stepped out of his path and continued on to the hotel's conference hall.

Her boss was waiting to see how her announcement

was received. This was the most important day of her career, and she needed his blessing to proceed with the next phase of her research.

It was research that couldn't be done in her lab, her office, or some centuries-old and dusty library. No, it would need to be in the field where she worked best. If he turned her down, then this was potentially her last day as a fellow at the London Conservatory.

But after just a few steps, with her focus back to the notecard in her hand; she smacked into a hard wall of muscle. *"Oof!"* Sucking in a breath from the sudden impact, her gaze landed on a pair of large combat boots, then traveled up the very big, and very tall beyond fit body of the man blocking her path. The guy had muscles on top of muscles.

When she reached his chest, she focused on his clothing. He wore a dark-gray, long-sleeved Henley that molded his upper body like a second skin, snug black cargo pants, and a wicked-looking sword strapped to his back. He unnervingly reminded her of a modern-day Highlander.

"Pardon me, I'm so sorry." She moved to step around him, but he slid sideways, blocking her. Unease flowed through her, then incredibly a full-body punch of desire unlike anything she'd ever felt washed through her. Dazed, she scanned the area behind him. Damn. They were alone in the hallway.

At the dual hit to her warring senses, her gaze snapped back to his face. The man's sharp, chiseled features and long, white-silvery hair was twisted at the temples in intricate braids, then severely pulled back. Her breath hitched as she locked into his narrowed eyes. Their color, an intense black with a line of dark green around the irises.

But that wasn't the most bizarre part. Not by a mile. That was reserved for an instant flash of light that pulsed from his eyes as their gazes held. Britt couldn't look away. Nor could she deny that the words he spoke a moment ago had been meant to intimidate her.

The behemoth blocking her meant to do her harm. Her heartbeat spiked as the thought raced through her, as yet another flush of intense warmth followed by an incredible need engulfed her. *What the hell was happening to her?*

As the thought formed, his gaze went from menacing to wide-eyed confusion, the corners of his mouth turning downward.

Then she swore she heard him say, "Tis not possible."

Without warning, the stranger pushed her up against the wall, and the clear evidence of a shift in his previous intent toward her became undeniably clear. And it was pressed against her abdomen.

Raising her arms to fend him off proved useless. One of his heavily muscled arms wound around her waist, trapping her left arm as he pulled her into his hard, unyielding body. His heat overwhelming, it sent thousands of electrical jolts through her as she tried to push against him. The too-intimate contact fogged her brain: drug-like yet overwhelmingly pleasant.

"Listen, I think...you have me mistaken...with someone else. I—" Her voice sounded super relaxed, like she'd just had a couple glasses of wine.

Just then, the man's other massive hand cradled the back of her head as he continued staring into her eyes. Unmoving, he appeared hypnotized. What was going on?

Terror seized her, and the implications of his attack finally sank in. Had someone sent him to steal her work? Years of sacrifice and research had led her to this moment. So, yeah, not happening. Whatever she had to do, she'd do. Taking in a calming breath, she pushed the panic aside. She needed to escape. Now.

Then Britt did the first thing that came to mind and stomped on his foot with the heel of her shoe. Lifting a knee, she aimed it toward his groin; it was a long shot considering their height difference. Screw it, it was her best option. But she froze before she could strike when she noticed the sword was now in his hand.

A sword with a very long, very sharp blade that emitted an ethereal glow. Mesmerized by the blade's beauty more so than its wicked intent, yet her scientific instinct was to identify the provenance of its origins. Such ancient items were her specialty—what she'd once been paid to locate—before her time at the conservatory.

Scream. Scream the building down, Britt. As she heeded her internal command, she took a breath to scream but ended up inhaling an earthy scent mingled with a bite of the sea. It overwhelmed her and prevented her scream from forming.

Incredibly, his scent relaxed her; imprinted itself into her pores. It was familiar—but not. She was positive she'd never encountered it before today.

Her gaze slammed into his. His eyes were no longer black, but a deep, dark green, several shades darker than her own pale green. And his expression matched the shock she felt.

Both now frozen, neither one of them seemed able to look away. Seconds ticked by before the wanna-be Highlander let loose a growl; its vibration resonated in her core, and her stomach dipped at the tenor of his voice.

Confused by her reaction and his, she was robbed of the opportunity to defend herself as he recovered first, propelling them toward the hotel's main exit. Struggling to get out his hold did little good. He had to outweigh her by close to seventy, maybe eighty pounds.

She fought his hold to no avail. Sure, he was MMA big, but she worked out and kept her body in top physical condition. She'd spent most of her life preparing for danger, but until this very moment, she hadn't had to put her years of training to the test.

Why today of all days? Her chance at the much-needed funding slipped away with each step taken in the opposite direction.

"Lass, you need to understand two things straight off. One, I'm stronger than you, and two, you now belong to me. And three, your lecturing days are over."

The sound of his voice elicited another spark of

awareness. Ignoring her body's reaction, she tested his first theory again and wrenched her arm. *Ow!* Okay, so he's strong, freakishly so. As for his second point, he couldn't have been more wrong.

"That's three things, you...you, you oaf! You obviously have the wrong woman. Perhaps I look like whoever you were searching for, but I can assure you I would remember if we'd met before. I never forget an asshole."

"This is not a case of mistaken identity, Dr. Harmony. You're the senior archeologist for the Ancient Artifact Conservatory of London. You graduated from Yale with honors in archeology and a minor in mythology, and you're on your way to not only convince your boss that you need funding to go back into the field, but to announce to the world at large about the discovery of a very important artifact. A scroll."

Britt's mouth dropped open. "How... how do you—"

Leaning down, he said, "Because it's my job to know. To protect." His breath whispered against her neck. This time her shivers had nothing to do with desire. Cold dread doused any warmth left in her body.

"Protect me?"

"No. The world."

Her heart skipped, and her body went from cold to ice at his words.

She wrenched her neck to look closer at him. Was he having a mental break? Possibly, but he looked straight out of central casting. Someone had to be pulling a prank on her. Yes, that's what this was. She'd seen signs for a movie audition in the hotel's lobby. A local production company was seeking an actor to portray the hero in a new show—a highlander.

Duh, men had been coming and going, wearing kilts of varying types of plaids, since she arrived from London yesterday. She'd even been hit on by a few of them in the bar last night. This one, although not wearing a kilt, was taking his role a bit too seriously.

Wait. Maybe someone had paid him to do this? Oh, God, was that it? She wouldn't have put it past Greg, her creep of a coworker, to orchestrate this farce as payback. "Jealous much" should have been the whiny researcher's middle name. At least he'd chosen a convincing actor. Too convincing, especially with that sword. Now safely behind his back again.

"Look, Mister. I'm not sure how much Greg paid you, but I'll double it if you go back and join your fellow actors. I don't have time to play. I'm the keynote—"

"Lass—"

"Doctor," I interrupted. Yes, the correction was petty, but damn it, she needed to have some control in this situation.

"Lass, I'm no actor, and I've never spoken to or met a man named Greg. Rest assured, every word I've said is truth."

Five minutes. That's all she had was five minutes until she needed to be at the lectern. Dammit. She would not miss her opportunity.

"Tell me who you are right now, why you're dragging me away from my job, or I will scream my head off."

Britt pleaded. She then pushed against his chest, hoping he'd release her. But he would not budge. The man was a solid mass of granite.

Instead of releasing her, he swept her up in his arms as if she were his bride. Her breath whooshed from her, hair fell over her eyes, and she was momentarily stunned. When she recovered, they were now just twenty feet from the hotel's exit.

In full panic mode, Britt frantically searched for someone to help her. But he pulled her tighter against his chest so that even if she wanted to scream, she couldn't take a full breath. Reality doubled down, and cold sweat enveloped her.

Britt managed to let out a weak, "Help me, please?" A lot of good that did. Then she noticed a group of older women heading toward the reception desk, and she tried again to call out. This time was weaker than the first. And it didn't slow him down. It only made him peer down at her, eyes narrowed, but it had the opposite effect on her of what he was probably going for.

Her body broke out in goosebumps. No! What was wrong with her? A vibration rumbled from his chest, followed by a growl so low she wasn't sure if she imagined it or not. His eyes flashed bright once again, then in a nanosecond returned to normal.

He held her gaze, leaving her briefly immobile. *What was that?* And wouldn't it be just her luck that anyone paying attention to them would probably think he was comforting her instead of kidnapping her?

With sheer willpower, she tore her gaze from him.

They were now just steps away from the exit. She looked around in one last attempt to find help. Looking out through the hotel's front windows, she noticed a man outside who equaled her kidnapper in height and girth, standing next to a dirt-covered Land Rover. He lifted a hand, and her kidnapper returned the signal with a nod.

Shit. With every ounce of her remaining strength, it had to be now or never; she bucked wildly and began rocking against his body.

"Lass, I need you to calm down! Once we're outside, I'll explain further. But right now—"

"Fuck calm. You're not taking me anywhere." Triumph filled her as his grip loosened. Ready to scream her head off, she opened her mouth.

His lips descended onto hers.

She hadn't even seen him move until it was too late.

And now she was lost to his sensual onslaught.

CHAPTER
TWO

The kiss turned surprisingly soft as he stroked his tongue across her lips. And in a moment of recklessness, Britt let him kiss her, believing she could use it as a distraction to her advantage.

Except she miscalculated. His scent affected her as before; her body relaxed and melted into his. And she took all he gave. Their tongues dueling, her breathing sped up. She inched closer to him, but then he lifted his head. Despair filled her at the loss.

And then for one precious moment she read doubt in his eyes. But then he blew her world apart and started walking again.

"Now, Lass. I'll only do this one more time. I know how much you enjoy me carrying you across thresholds, but 'tis the last time. Having you so close gives me too many ideas, and I don't want to embarrass these nice folks." His heavily accented voice boomed, carrying a hint of sensuality.

His words broke her out of the weird spell she'd fallen under, and Britt watched in amazement as a smile split his face before he made a show of looking at a few people who finally stopped to watch the spectacle before moving on.

What was it with this guy? She shook her head to ward off the unwelcome sexual desire. This man meant her harm no matter what she felt, no matter what she thought she saw in his gaze. No matter how devastatingly thorough his kiss was.

"Ugh. No one believes your bullshit. Put me down." Did he think anyone with a lick of sense would believe such nonsense?

"Look around, lass, no one seems concerned."

She looked, and he was right. Except for the doorman, who was grinning and propping the revolving doors open so they could pass through, no one paid them any attention or were coming to her aid.

If he got her in that car... no, it would not happen. He halted next to the Rover and set her down.

"The name is Quinn Smythe. This is my brother Roane--"

Before she could talk herself out of it, she kicked him, or tried to knee him in the groin. He was too damn tall. She connected with his thigh, totally ineffective. And to make her situation even worse, she lost her balance. Saved from really hurting herself, he caught her arm and pulled her into his side just in time.

"I'm only going to tell you once, Lass—no kicking. It's not ladylike."

"Well, good thing I'm no lady, asshole." Britt turned her growing anger into another attempt at freedom, pushed off his chest, getting loose, then turned to run. But before she could take a second step, she slammed into a granite wall. His friend had moved, blocking her only hope of escape.

"Quinn. You're not going to let this slip of a woman best you, are you?" Roane asked, his voice full of humor.

Britt assessed her situation. Gone was any hope of making it back into the symposium, triumphantly presenting her findings, and hopefully securing more funding to continue her career-long quest to find the mythical Emerald Tablets.

She clutched the strap of her messenger bag, which had thankfully stayed put during her ordeal, praying they didn't ask for it. She hadn't been forced into the car —yet. A spark of hope filled her.

Scanning the area for another option to get away from them, a couple exited the hotel walking toward their waiting car. She shouted to them but got no further than "Hey!" and Quinn lifted a hand toward the couple. Britt gasped as a shimmering wave of pulsed through the air toward them.

She shouted again, but they ignored her and climbed in the car and drove off.

"What the hell did you do to them?" She lifted her face to Quinn. "What was that?"

He shrugged his shoulders. "They'll be fine. I sent a

wave of energy, effectively making us invisible. Now, please get in the Rover with no more kicking, hmm?"

She looked between Quinn and his brother. Their expressions unconcerned with her distress, as if they kidnapped women every day. She'd already tried and failed at running, so there was no other choice but to resort to a weapon she loathed to use. Tears. "Please. Let me go. I won't tell anyone. I promise." She sniffed and wiped away a tear off her chin.

Quinn's partner in crime looked at her with the oddest expression, considering her performance was spot on—in her opinion. Perhaps he'd never seen a woman cry before. She snorted. Considering his good looks, she found that hard to believe. Men like them wouldn't lack for female companionship, and if they'd met under different circumstances, perhaps she and Quinn could... oh, my God. Now she was fantasizing about hooking up with him? *Get a hold of yourself, Britt.*

"Enough. You have something we want, nay need, and your fake tears are useless, lass."

"Quinn?" Roane interrupted.

"Get in the car without another outburst, and once inside, perhaps we can negotiate—"

"Negotiate? There is nothing to negotiate except letting me go."

"Quinn. I really need you to—"

Ignoring Roane, he once again took her by the elbow, opened the door, and nudged her inside. Freedom disappeared as Britt crawled inside the ancient Rover.

Quinn followed her in, grabbed her thigh as she

scrambled for the opposite door holding her in place so she could no longer move, and latched the seatbelt over her lap. His brisk movements still managed to turn her on, despite the realization that she was well and truly trapped.

"Safety first." His eyes flashed that eerie green, and without taking his gaze off her, he said, "Drive."

THREE

Roane guided the ancient Rover away from valet parking and onto the main road. She whipped her head around and gazed at the front of the building where she'd thought she'd be announcing her greatest triumph.

Not in her wildest dreams did she think she'd be leaving in such a manner. Certainly not kidnapped, kissed, and manhandled by a man better suited for an epic movie than real life.

"You're nuts. You both are if you think you can just take me like this. Look, I meant it when I said I'll tell no one. I need to give this speech. Over a hundred of the world's top archeologists came here specifically to hear what I have to say."

A muscle ticked in his jaw. She watched in fascination as his green eyes darkened back to black and his full lips thinned. Lips she had firsthand knowledge of and suddenly wanted to taste again.

On the verge of real tears, Britt looked out the side window, watching the cityscape of Inverness whiz past as they left the storied city and headed toward the famed highlands. A strangled laugh erupted from her. Never let them take you to another location. That's how you get dead. She blew that one big time.

"We have no plans to kill you, lass. Quite the opposite. Now."

Quinn responded to her as if she'd spoken the thought aloud. Perhaps she had. Perhaps she was going mad. They were all mad.

"Now? Oh my God, you are crazy. You two are certifiable if you think you can get away with this. Someone will report what they saw. I'm sure there were surveillance cameras and... ugh, I have rights, goddamn it, and being kidnapped and manhandled by you and the Rock is so not on the list of things to do while in Scotland."

She could have sworn Quinn's mouth tilted into the beginning of a grin before he schooled his features into an unreadable mask.

"Um, she's right about the kidnapping part, Quinn. That wasn't part of the plan."

"True. But plans change. It seems the Fates have come through at last." He turned his attention back to her. "Rest assured, the plan to...end you...is no more. And your role in assisting us, and mankind, has begun."

"End me?" She stiffened. What the hell did fate or the Fates, whatever, have to do with any of this?

Perhaps they really had suffered a psychotic break.

But two at the same time? Maybe they were on drugs? Or maybe they'd somehow discovered she'd not only found proof the tablets existed, but that she'd recovered a small piece of one?

Quinn hadn't broken eye contact with her since he'd pushed her into the backseat. She couldn't look away either. His energy and scent pulling her in, and she felt perpetually turned-on by him. Yet, underneath the instant sensual connection, Britt assessed her situation. It would quickly go from bad to epically bad if she didn't figure out how to get herself out of the vehicle.

Not that being kidnapped wasn't bad, but deep down, she knew her world would never be the same if she allowed herself to see how the situation played out, no matter how much her abdomen fluttered for Quinn.

A cough sounded from the driver's compartment. Then another.

"Aye?" Quinn responded to his brother.

"So, what, now I'm a guest? Well, heck, where's my complimentary glass of champagne?" Her sarcasm was ignored. She could really use a drink—anything to take the edge off.

"Quinn. Does this mean what I think it means. Is she...is she yours?"

"It's why she's with us and," Quinn's words broke off with a strangled croak.

Britt stared at herself in the mirror and watched as her reflection paled. She sat back, closed her eyes, and prayed.

Weariness descended, and she chanced a peek at the

imposing man who held her life in his hands. Quinn was still staring at her. Instead of the perma-scowl he'd worn since this farce had begun, his face now held regret as he studied her.

"...and It's what kept me from taking her life." His words were directed to Roane while he looked at her.

Now there's a string of words she'd never heard before. Instead of succumbing to a full freak-out, she shook her head and laughed. She followed up by reciting every curse word she knew.

Somewhere between "asshat" and "motherfuckers," he'd shifted his large frame closer his thigh brushing hers. She reacted by scooting closer to the door, but not before she'd felt another zap of awareness, the electricity of the touch overwhelming. She cringed at her body's response as she looked for answers in his too-handsome face.

Britt had been aware from a very young age what would occur if the wrong, or maybe the right person, discovered her...talent.

Her destiny had been told to her by her father in the guise of a made-up fairy tale. That the little princess in his story, that her birth had been anticipated for generations, that she would be one of a very few that would change the world.

She never believed it, not really. Although her special skills should have given her a clue, the fairy tale had been buried with her father when he'd been taken from Britt at a young age.

Out of ideas, she decided to plead for reason, but instead, an earsplitting concussion exploded around them, and everything went silent.

CHAPTER
FOUR

Quinn threw his body over hers, and she heard Roane yell.

"Midnight Riders on our six." Roane turned the air blue and began driving in a weaving pattern which made her stomach roil.

Quinn lifted his head and stared out the rear window. "More like the second string."

Her gaze flashed back to the rearview mirror. A Humvee on steroids hugged their tail along with two motorcycles. Each carried a passenger holding weapons. Britt curled her fingers around the cracked leather seat. Was she in a movie, and no one had bothered to tell her?

"Faster, man," Quinn bellowed.

Their speed increased. Quinn reached under the bench seat. "Lift your feet." He pulled out an army-green cylindrical piece of metal she'd only seen in movies.

It was a grenade launcher.

She'd been sitting on top of a fucking grenade launcher this entire time. "Who the hell are you?" Panic lacing her demand.

Quinn ignored her and readied the weapon, then hefted it to his shoulder. She had no time to be terrified.

"Get down on the floor and cover your head."

He didn't have to tell her twice. Quinn stood up through the retractable roof, aimed, and fired. She ducked down into a tight ball and covered her head with her arms. Time stood still. She recited a prayer her father had instilled in her from childhood and waited.

An earthshaking blast rocked the Rover. Her hands slammed over her ears in a failed attempt to protect them from the ensuing ear-piercing boom.

A roar of triumph came from the driver's seat, quickly followed by another blast erupting behind them. Men yelled. Screams of pain rang out. She was in the middle of a goddamned war zone.

"Damn, Quinn. Your aim's improving. The Humvee's toast, but the idiots on the cycles are still pursuing. Say the word, and I'll do a one-eighty if you want to go one-on-one."

Roane's words sent a chill through her—and not the good kind.

Quinn descended through the roof's opening. His gaze slammed into hers. His natural scowl was still in place, yet its intensity warmed her to her toes.

"No. We can't chance they'll take the lass if we let them get too close."

"Hey, the lass has a name. And a doctorate," she

mumbled to herself. Crawling up on her knees she took her first look at the chaos behind them. Puffs of white smoke scattered along the pavement, and the charred Humvee weaved drunkenly before it came to a rest. Flames shot out from every crack and crevice. The screams of their attackers had now gone silent.

Quinn ignored her and whipped off his shirt. She blinked. Twice. Three times as his biceps were revealed. A sleeveless t-shirt hugged his chest. Various markings wound around his arms and ended on his shoulders. Some tattoos looked Celtic; others resembled Egyptian hieroglyphs, but not. Her palms itched to trace them.

He flashed her a grin, and she froze. A scowling Quinn was something to be wary of. A smiling Quinn? Devastating. *Breathe, Britt. Just fucking breathe.*

As she continued to watch him, Quinn pulled a serrated knife from his waistband and hit a button to lower the rear window. A blast of acrid smoke filled the cabin.

"Shite. They're using chem bombs. Roane, toss a mask to Britt."

Tears formed, her eyes stung, and she gulped in a mouthful of the bitter smoke. Coughs wracked her body.

"Hold your breath until the mask is on. Understood?" Quinn's voice, for the first time since this total farce began, held something that sounded like he actually cared about her.

She nodded and wiped away the nonstop flow of tears. Grasping the mask, she followed Quinn's directions and placed the breather over her mouth, then sucked in fresh air. Kidnapped or not, an acute aware-ness of the danger she was in clicked into place, and she trembled. Her life was now in the hands of her kidnapper.

"You'll be fine as long as you do as I say. Got it?"

Nodding, because what could she do? Her lungs were full of poisonous gas. She hoped to God it would clear out as she continued taking slow, deep breaths. Her thoughts raced at what she saw. Oh. My. God. Men with horns—not men, demons—attacked them. Were still attacking them.

Fear slammed into her, and her heart threatened to explode from her chest. All of her plans were no longer hers to direct. They hadn't been since the moment the handsome highlander had stepped into her path.

Another series of pops sounded outside the vehicle. She adjusted her mask and resumed her position on the floor, then nodded at Quinn. He leaned down as if to comfort her but pulled back his hand. She hadn't been expecting softness from a man who'd killed others in their escape.

Without a word, he turned back to the fight and shouted at Roane for an update. She made herself relax by chanting a poem her father had written for her, and for the first time since Quinn grabbed her arm and carried her from the hotel, she felt safe.

Something told her he'd never hurt her. She was going to hold on to that feeling with everything she had and pray to those who came before her that everything would work out.

"They're falling back," Roane shouted.

"What?" Quinn barked.

"They've retreated. Maybe they realized we're too smart to let them take us out."

Quinn shook his head. "No. Dante's forces wouldn't give up so easily. He commands them to fight to the death. Ours or theirs."

"What if it's not his band of idiots? Should we consider that someone else knows about her?" Roane asked.

Quinn's gaze pierced hers. "Do you know of anyone who would want you dead?"

"Besides you? Gee, let me think... uh, no."

He ignored her sarcasm but not her words. "You no longer need fear me or any of the Brethren. Your life is vital to our mission. And to me. Rest assured, we'll see you safely out of this."

"Right. You expect me to take your word on that and just go along without any..." Brit's eyes widened, her words forgotten as a scream rent the air. Hers. Through the window behind Quinn appeared a black object. A big, black helicopter beelined for them, outlined in stark contrast to the pink and red hues of the setting sun.

Guns aimed directly at them. Check that—cannons mounted on its rails. "Mother of all that's holy. Who are these men, and why are they after us?"

FIVE

"That one-eighty would be appreciated. Now!" Quinn yelled at Roane.

The Rover rocked and tipped hard to the side as she was tossed closer to Quinn. Hands pushed her onto the floor. Quinn placed his body over hers. Britt absorbed his heat. She bit her lip to keep a moan from escaping. Her traitorous body couldn't get enough of him. If she hadn't known better, she would have accused him of drugging her. She'd had nothing to drink since he took her from the hotel, and she would have felt a needle prick. Her reactions made no sense.

In deference to her roller-coaster emotions, he was calm yet energized. As if kidnapping women, using magic, and fighting demons were a normal day for them. They seemed to be in their element. And she wanted nothing to do with it.

"Hell, Quinn. They've upgraded. You're going to have

to bring out the big guns. Looks like whoever this is wants your mate, and bad."

Britt froze. Mate? She pushed at the muscled wall above her. Nothing, not even an inch of freedom. "Let me up!" Her demand went ignored. Wiggling her feet, she could free her left foot, but that was it. Her human prison was too big, too heavy to escape. It had become a prison she was enjoying just a bit too much as a zap of electricity hit her abdomen when her backside brushed a hardness between his legs.

"Lass. Stop moving now." His low tone held a mixture of warning edged with lust.

He may wield power and a life force unknown and superior to hers, but she wasn't about to let a stranger rule her body or her destiny. If this were to be her last day, she was going out on her own terms.

She tensed each muscle and bucked her body. Her action produced a low growl from Quinn and a heavy dose of frustration within her. The vehicle came to a sudden halt, and she tried again, desperate for freedom. He didn't budge an inch; instead, he ground himself into her and whispered, "Later."

That one word was all it took to melt her. He lifted himself up and off her, and she scrambled up and rounded on him, pushing her hair out of her eyes. Full of rage at her inability to escape, she opened her mouth to demand her release. But his gaze held her still, and she was once again filled with need. For him.

Promise swam in his eyes as he swept her form, setting off mini-fireworks everywhere his gaze touched her. Britt shivered and did the unimaginable. She swayed toward him. Need overtook her good sense, and all she wanted was to feel his touch. In an instant, his scowl returned, and he was back in battle mode, shooting out of the Rover, barking out instructions to Roane.

What the hell was that? Their contact broken, she shook her head to clear the haze of desire that had over-taken her—again. She stretched, releasing the kinks that had formed from crouching on the floorboard, and watched as he strode toward the rear and lifted the hatch door—mesmerized by his efficient and fluid movements. He moved remarkably gracefully for a man at least a foot taller than her five-foot-six. He removed an object she couldn't make out clearly.

The helicopter hovered over them. Time faded away.

Quinn stepped clear of the Rover, and Roane let out a low whistle.

She twisted toward Roane, but he nodded for her to turn back to Quinn.

Her heart stopped. The world went silent. Her captor's hair had come loose from its anchor and brushed his shoulders. She noticed small rips in his shirt that hadn't registered before. They could only have been created by bullets. Yet he didn't bleed.

He moved unhurt, full of swagger. His kilt rustled against his massive thighs. The grand landscape of the Scottish Lowlands behind him held her enthralled. He threw his head back, spread his arms wide, and opened his stance to match. His lips moved, but she was too far away to hear his words.

The object he'd removed from the back was now clasped in his right hand. It glinted in the setting sun as he stepped forward, directly under the helicopter. He held a sword. It was half his body length, and it emitted a green glow. Quinn roared and brought his hands together, thrusting the sword up and over his head. A beam of bright white light enveloped the steel bird. An explosion split the object into a hundred pieces.

Britt expected screams, yet she heard nothing except her own labored breathing and the sound of blood rushing in her ears. The sight before her was magnificent. Her attention was torn between the man and the sword he wielded. A need to possess both frightened and thrilled her. At that moment, she realized both man and sword were ancient; each held a power unfathomable to mankind.

And she'd witnessed too much.

Did he know who she was beyond the celebrated archeologist who'd found a secret most would die to behold? Did he know? That she, just like him, was more than human.

A deep need for him called to her. Growing up without a mother, she had no one to talk to about the silly girlhood dreams of a man like this one rescuing her from a life of darkness. Besides a short-lived romance in college, Britt had little experience with desires fulfilled. Her father's fairy tales had featured a descendant of a goddess; some labeled the beautiful woman a witch. She was the first female born in centuries in her father's line. He and those before him carried the magical Celtic blood destined to save mankind.

God, she'd never believed him. Never believed the fanciful tale of love, duty, and a war between gods and demons. Until today.

Quinn threw himself back into the Rover as bits of the destroyed helicopter and things she didn't want to spend too much time thinking on where, or whom they came from, rained down on the vehicle's roof.

Roane let out a yell of triumph. "*Aaand*, that's how it's done." He whipped the wheel and put them back on their original path. Her shoulder slammed against the door, and she gripped the handle. Two things happened at that moment. One, she realized the latch was no longer locked. And two, her instinct to flee almost overrode her need to discover the strange connection she had with Quinn.

Her hand shook in anticipation. Britt used her peripheral vision to gauge the changing landscape and noted Roane was no longer driving as if the Cerberus himself was nipping at their heels. The land, bathed in the remaining glow from the setting sun, should work in her favor.

She needed to keep her identity hidden—from everyone. She needed to save herself. Yet, she wanted to discuss the existence of otherworldly beings with Quinn. She would have to pursue that knowledge later. Much later.

"Lass, are you well?"

She turned to Quinn and swept her gaze over the man who, in less than thirty minutes, had kidnapped her and saved her. Despite her unruly hormones, her life being spared from creatures she'd only read about, and the best kiss she ever experienced, she'd rather take her chances in the wilds of Scotland than spend another moment with no say in her destiny.

"Screw you." Britt clutched her research to her breast, yanked open the door, and rolled onto the pavement.

"Fuck." Little surprised Quinn after almost six millennia; however, Britt had done so—twice. Her spirit during their initial moments together exhilarated him as no other woman had in his long life. She was unmatched in beauty and spirit, and she'd bested him by doing the unexpected.

"Shite. Sorry, I forgot to secure the doors." Roane executed another one-eighty and brought them to the spot where Britt had exited.

Quinn hit the ground running before Roane brought the vehicle to a sudden stop. Not only had he spent the last forty-eight hours staring at Britt's photo, memorizing every feature, but he'd also read her dossier and knew every detail of her life, and thought he'd come to know her. He was wrong.

Yes, she was an active person. Hobbies included hiking, scuba diving, and reading everything from the collected works by ancient Greek writers to happily-ever-afters, but jumping out of speeding vehicles hadn't been included.

"Head north," Roane shouted.

Quinn corrected direction and scanned a patch of overgrown brush. Darkness had fallen, yet his eyesight adapted. He could see as well as if it were noon. They were twenty miles from the castle, but if he didn't get her back and under his protection, the demons, undoubtedly sent by Dante, would be all over her.

The Duke of Hell's fingerprints were all over the demons who'd attacked them. The underworld master of manipulation had added arms dealer to his long resume shortly after the human's last world war. His operation centered in Arizona had long been suspected to be near to an opening to hell hidden from the humans and the Brethren. Their brother, Trace, guarded the Americas and he'd recently pinpointed an area in the desert blanketed by magic. They were close to discovering and destroying Dante's breach between the two realms.

Today's attempt on Britt all but confirmed the Fates' centuries-old prophecy had begun because like the Brethren, Dante had discovered Britt's existence.

Urgency rode Quinn hard. If she were indeed his mate, as he was almost certain based on their instant physical connection, finding her and keeping her from Dante's brutal hands was his only priority.

"Britt. Show yourself." His footfalls increased when he saw her dash into a prickly grove of burdock. Was the woman daft? She'd be torn to shreds by the brambles, and now that he was aware of who she could be to him, the thought of one scratch on her delicate skin tightened his gut.

A quick scan of the surrounding area found just two other life signatures, Roane's and hers. He heard a low mumbling and followed it through the thick brush. She was cursing him and the greenery. He picked up the scent of blood, and panic slammed into him. "Britt, we need to get to my castle. I know you're scared, but you're safer with me."

"Scared? Ha. First, what I am is pissed. My lungs hurt, and I itch—all over. What is this stuff? And last, why would I willingly go anywhere with you? I could have been killed back there."

Quinn zeroed in on her location and eased his way within feet. The breeze had picked up, the temperature had dropped, and he was done trying to coax the female out of the brush. "Aye. We all could have. But I've learned you rarely turn down a challenge. And I've one to issue. I have answers to questions I'm sure you'll be pestering me with once we're safe."

No response.

"I promise no harm will come to you..." He arrived at the spot where he was certain she hid. Matted leaves marked her presence, but no Britt. He looked up, and from the corner of his eye, he caught a flash. Somehow, she'd freed herself and was now scrambling up a small hill.

Damn this woman. Not that he had much experience

with them beyond fulfilling his baser needs, but she was proving herself to be smarter than any female he'd encountered. He grinned—finally, someone to challenge him.

She lost her footing and slid backward. He caught her ankle and an eyeful of her shapely backside. Her hair windblown and dotted with brambles.

"No, please. Let me go." Her plea touched him deep.

He didn't want her to fear him, but there was no other way to secure her safety.

She kicked out with her free foot, clipped his chin, and regained her footing. However, she only gained a couple of feet up the hill before he landed on top of her. But she wasn't done fighting. She twisted her torso and attempted to kick him again. He wound his arms around her waist and flipped them, landing on his back with her sprawled on top. He locked his arms around her as she tried and failed to escape. Now chest to breast, he held her gaze, their breaths mingling, and marveled at the woman in his arms.

His gaze swept down to her half-exposed breasts, and his cock grew with each passing second. Gods, she was perfect for him. Curves and long dark locks perfect for wrapping his hands around, and... he expelled a low growl. Her continued movements were creating a friction he could stand for only so long.

"Let. Me. Go." Britt's tone was neither pleading nor cajoling. It now held a determination he admired. He found it and her compelling. If they were true mates, neither could deny the other or their true wants and desires—at least once they'd joined in heart and the marriage bed. Until then, she would be vulnerable.

Another wiggle against his shaft, a brush of her breasts against his heated skin, he gritted his teeth and swore. Earlier, he'd sensed her arousal, so how was she unaware of his condition? How was she not as affected as he? This was no place to claim her, if she were his, and if he was willing to follow a prophecy that had failed the Brethren before.

How long had it been since he'd had a woman? Too damn long if he was becoming turned-on by a mere scuffle with a woman he'd known but an hour. However, she was not any female.

And a lot had happened in that hour. He was very well holding his destined mate. She could belong to Roane, Mac, Trace, Keir or Gavin. His body tensed at the thought, and his instinct to protect, to fight for what's his, slammed into him.

Deep in his soul, he already knew the truth. His feelings had turned soon after touching her. He'd been ready to end this woman's life based on her intention to reveal to the humans what the Brethren had been tasked to prevent. The existence of the fabled Emerald Tablets was true. And if she had given her speech to a roomful of scientists and investors, eventually the world would learn of the Brethren as well.

Quinn breathed deep through his nose and cursed his sire. How much did she know about the tablets? And would the bond of the prophecy, once enacted, keep her safe?

"Britt, stop struggling. Take a moment and listen. The longer we're out here, the easier it will be for Dante and his crew to locate us—you. I will provide the answers you seek, plus an opportunity for you to become more than you dreamed. I have access to great relics. Relics you have been searching for."

He felt her go still at the mention of relics. Finally, he'd gotten through to her. She let out a squeak as she settled on top of him. Ah, she found his reaction to her. He should use that against her, but they were exposed and without backup or his sword. And they'd run out of time.

"Ah, so this is what, bribery? A proposition to stay silent about your hidden talents in exchange for a look at some dusty old pottery? No thanks. I'll take my chances with what's-his-name."

"He goes by Dante these days. He's a Duke of Hell who controls legions of demons and bespelled humans who do his bidding, preying on others in his quest for absolute rule. And when I say humans, think terrorists."

"Rule over what?" she whispered.

"Heaven, hell, everything and everyone on Earth."

Britt responded with a snort and started twisting again. He closed his eyes and swore once again to his creator. His patience gone, he tightened his hold.

"Lass, you keep that up, and you're not going to like my next move. Now stop and promise me you won't run off again."

"I'm just trying to get away from that, er your—"

He gritted his teeth and let out a low chuckle. "I can assure you one thing, Britt. When you're near, that part of me will always struggle for dominance. Now, promise me."

Quinn sensed her fear and inner turmoil. Her life was about to change, hell it had already, and it was a lot for anyone to take in. Yet, he needed her agreement, so they could move on and solve the problem she'd created. "I suppose you'll keep following me no matter where I go?"

"You'll not get far. That I can guarantee."

He felt her shudder and take in a deep breath before she sighed.

"Fine. But I do so under protest. The only reason I'm agreeing is to find out those answers you promised me. When I'm satisfied, we're done, and you'll let me go. Deal?"

"Lass, you'll never be satisfied. It's not in your nature. But when we're...done, I give you my promise you will be free to do as you wish."

"Right, like you know my nature. But...okay, I promise. I won't run again. But that doesn't mean I won't defend myself if I feel threatened."

She pushed against his hold. Quinn loosened his arms, allowing her to stand. His gaze followed her movements as she brushed dirt off her clothes. When her hands passed over her perfect ass, he didn't hide his groan. She sent him a glare, and at his nod, she began walking back to the Rover.

Confident in the deal they'd made, his smile widened, enjoying not only her spirit but the sway of her hips. He waited a moment to follow her, allowing his body's reaction to cool down.

Little did she realize he would never be done with her.

SEVEN

The sudden stop of the Rover snapped Britt from her whirling thoughts. Rubbing the grit from her eyes, she peered out into the blackness of the highlands. She jumped out and surveyed the desolate landscape and some castle ruins lit by the Rover's headlights. Crashing waves and the smell of the sea slammed into her senses.

"Nice castle. You rent it off Airbnb?"

He once again ignored her sarcasm. Instead of picking a fight with her, which was what she secretly wanted, he waved his arm; an energy wave shimmered, similar to the one he created at the hotel when he'd messed with the crowd's heads.

In an instant, ancient ruins which had stood sentry to a past long forgotten became a fully intact castle. Not a stone was missing. It had two towers on each end and a massive, weathered, wooden double door. And it had a freaking moat.

Her imagination flashed on an image of a knight in full battle armor astride his horse, breaching the entrance. Quinn was that knight or highlander.

She blinked once, then twice to clear her vision. Yup, it was still there. A moat and an honest-to-goodness draw bridge. It creaked as it lowered. "What? How?"

"There are more things in heaven and earth, Horatio, than are dreamt of in your philosophy." Quinn recited Shakespeare's famous line from Hamlet perfectly.

"So, I'm learning," she whispered. She turned back toward him, taking in a steadying breath. "I can't wait to hear your explanation, but I'm tired and itchy. You wouldn't happen to have hot running water and a bathtub in there, would you?"

"Aye, we may live in a thousand-year-old castle, but it has all the modern amenities. I could use a shower as well. Let's go in, and I'll show you to your room. After your bath, we'll eat a hot meal and then discuss... matters."

Quinn turned to Roane, who hadn't said a word since her ill-fated escape and seemed to only speak when necessary. "Will you be staying the night?"

"No. I've my own business to attend. Besides, I sense Mac is within. He'll be chaperone enough until the binding ceremony." Roane turned to Britt and gave a short bow. "It's been a pleasure. Welcome to the family."

Before Britt could wrap her head around the phrase "binding ceremony," he'd sent her a wink and walked off into the surrounding field, then disappeared. She felt her forehead. No fever. She pinched her arm. Pain erupted.

"You wouldn't happen to have any whiskey in there, would you?"

Quinn had begun to walk toward the now-lowered drawbridge. "Is the Pope Catholic, lass? Besides, in Scotland, whiskey is the national drink."

His burr had deepened. It sent a thrill through her. Number twelve since she'd met him, at least. *Kidnapped Britt, the man kidnapped you.* Don't romanticize the situation.

He offered her his arm and a rare smile. A small one, but it still counted. He led her over the bridge. The doors opened on their own. Quinn gave a push inside. She stopped inside the threshold and stared. A great room greeted them. Its modern features belied the structure that had appeared moments ago. An enormous fireplace swallowed the opposite wall. She felt its warmth from where they stood.

Her exhaustion forgotten, she broke free of Quinn and explored the room. She took in the smell of peat from the fire and drank in the mix of new and antique furnishings. A full bar sat to the left of the fireplace, and an overstuffed leather couch sat in a half circle in the middle of the room facing it. Her gaze landed on a man-sized frosted window to her right. She noted there was no latch. A possible exit?

Before she took two steps to investigate further, Quinn's booming voice froze her in place.

"Lass, you'll find no escape. The castle's wired with motion sensors. And my own senses are attuned to your every move. Every exit, window, and mousehole is tied into the grid. I'll know the moment you breach the perimeter."

How had he'd known her intent? Well, hell, in the future, she'd do a better job of schooling her features. Tired and defeated, she sank into the cool leather and stared into the flames.

A third male appeared from an arched doorway to the left of the fireplace, wearing a welcoming smile. There were more of them?

Quinn grunted a welcome. The man matched Quinn in size, but that's where the similarity ended. His jet-black hair was short, and his eyes the darkest brown she'd ever seen. His cheekbones, high and prominent, his chin dimpled, and like Quinn and Roane, he was movie-star handsome.

Her highlander closed the distance between them and stood at the mantle, capturing her gaze.

"Britt, this is Mac. He's our tech expert."

Wait, "her highlander?" Why couldn't she shake the unwelcome urge to crawl all over the man? Attraction was one thing. This soul-deep connection between them shook her. It made no sense. She didn't believe in love at first sight, or fated mates or whatever. At least not since her father was killed right in front of her when she was ten. Life had become a daily struggle, and fairy tales were for books. On that day, she quickly learned the truth behind her father's tales of adventure, finding one's true love and good always conquering evil. They were fairy tales, nothing but made-up fantasies she almost thought were real.

And his promises of discovering the meaning behind her special gift as they traveled the world would never come true. The dreams that plagued her around the anniversary of his death had recently begun. And the demons from today's attack had triggered memories of the monsters that had brutally taken him from her. The similarities were—

"Lass, you okay?"

Shaking free from the memory fog, Britt focused her gaze on Mark—no, Mac. "I'd say it's a pleasure to meet you, but I'm all out of niceties at the moment." She turned her attention back to Quinn. He was the very picture of a laird of the castle as he stood in front of the fire. A fierce warrior, leader of his clan. She must remember he was the man who'd stolen her from her life.

She read an unspoken challenge and a hint of wicked intent in his gaze. His broad shoulders, thickly muscled arms, and tree-trunk-sized thighs created a warm tingle in her abdomen. He emitted an undeniable sensuality that ignited a deep ache within her.

His size hadn't intimidated her before and didn't now, but the way he was staring at her did. She rubbed her arms, attempting to end the connection between them. Quinn followed her movements which enflamed her further. Dammit.

Instead of thinking up ways to escape, she was mesmerized. Compelled to learn every inch of him; commit his features to memory.

He had a square jaw with a hint of a dimple and

the darkest green eyes she'd ever seen. Odd. Few people in the world possessed green eyes, and if they did, like her, the shade was often light or more hazel. Not his. His were dynamic, and the color changed often, depending on his mood. And his hair —silver, long, and tied back from his sculpted, handsome face. The silver color had thrown her at first. Its shade seemed natural, yet it couldn't be from old age. He couldn't be older than maybe mid-thirties. He was the most striking male she'd ever met.

"Forgive her, Mac. She's had quite the day. I still have much to tell her of our... mission." He spoke to his... brother, without breaking eye contact. It was incredibly sexy, and a reminder of how dangerous the situation she was in had become.

She couldn't afford to fall under his spell. A new desperation to flee gripped her hard. Not because she feared for her life, but for her self-respect. How crazy was it that she'd begun lusting for her captor?

"Lass, I'll have your word you'll not try to escape."

She rolled her eyes. As if she wouldn't try at every opportunity. His statement spurred her to double her efforts to resist the pull between them. She had to remember all she'd been through in such a short time. Living through a battle where she'd witnessed tech-nology that shouldn't exist, and watching men, or demons if he was to be believed, dying.

"Today's confrontation with Dantalion's men was just the opening shot. They'll come back for you, lass. Of that, I'm sure. You must agree that staying is your best and only option."

She'd about had it with his demanding personality. "Dammit, I have a name. I'm not your 'lass.' I'm Dr. Britt Harmony, and if that's too much for you to remember, you can call me Dr. But don't pretend an intimacy between us that's not there."

Quinn was next to her in an instant, leaning his heavily muscled arms on the top edge of the couch, effectively creating a cage—a very sexy cage.

"Ah, lass, I like our situation no better than you. This is not how I thought we'd meet. However, the Fates have chosen. To be presented with a mate as the conflict with the demons ramps up is the last thing I, nay we, need."

Britt had stopped listening after Quinn said "mate." She had to have misunderstood. The hairs on the back of her neck rose, and an allover body flush overcame her, chilling her to the bone. How quickly her life had turned into a nightmare.

Mac cleared his throat. "I hate to interrupt, but Gavin is here."

Their gazes were still locked, the air charged between them. Quinn's eyes flashed bright, unnaturally so, an instant before he hung his head. He growled before pushing off the couch and away from her.

The growl threw her. It sounded...animalistic, territorial even, and yet she instantly missed the intimacy of the moment. How messed up was that?

"Why didn't he greet us? Where is he?" Quinn looked behind Mac and frowned.

"Well, he's... resting?" Mac answered.

"Resting? Damn it. Serves him right. He was always too quick to act."

Another one? "Uh, hello. Still here. Let's get back to this mate thing you're referring to because I'm sure you don't mean me?" Britt asked.

Both men focused their gazes on her after a shared look passed between them that shook her.

"It's complicated." Quinn sighed.

"All the best stories are." Britt crossed her arms and sank deeper into the couch. Her messenger bag poked her. At least she still had the scroll. And her cell phone.

Maybe she had an escape plan after all.

EIGHT

Britt blocked everything and everyone out as she debated a new strategy. She needed to get alone. And she needed a bath after hiding, then rolling around in those damn bushes.

"It's part of the story I need to share with you. But right now, one of my brethren—"

Quinn's words finally penetrated through her plotting. "One of? How many are there?"

Her kidnapper sighed. "This will go a lot faster if you'd stop interrupting... Britt."

The use of her name produced tingles at the top of her thighs. She did her best to ignore the awareness Quinn created by finally using her given name. "How many?" She needed to know what she was up against.

Silence.

She turned Mac. "Will you tell me?"

Mac shook his head.

She tamped down a scream. "So, you're going to

keep that a secret from me too, even with all the things I've witnessed today? That's where you draw the line? Incredible."

"Some things are not up for discussion. At least until after we're bound."

She leaned forward, held her head, closed her eyes, and counted to ten. To twenty. To thirty. She was on her way to forty when Roane entered with an unconscious man over his shoulders.

"What happened?" Britt asked, worry lacing her tone.

"Portal sickness. He must not have spent enough time recharging between jumps," Roane huffed out. "Damn, he weighs a ton. Why he didn't go through in his other form...what had he been thinking?"

"Um, what other form?" Did she really want to know after all that had happened? "Why would he need to recharge? And portal sickness...what are you talking about?" Images from the day bombarded her as she tried to make sense of the senseless.

Britt snapped her gaze to Roane. "Wait a minute. I saw you disappear outside. How did you...." Had she fallen down a rabbit hole and ended up in another world, or maybe someone had slipped something into her room service coffee this morning. She'd accept that more easily than believing these men used portals and were able to change their form.

Dazed, she studied the men closely. What was she missing? Quinn's abilities and their advanced weaponry, plus the undeniable vibe connecting her to the now-silent, silver-haired man. Even now, as fear was riding her, her body was still on a low burn for him. Again, her father's fairy tales of destiny and the battle for humanity tickled her brain.

She needed the truth. Now.

If the men that'd attacked them were truly demons, then what were they? Before she could ask, Roane looked to Quinn, seeming to wait for permission.

Quinn shook his head at the unspoken question.

So that's how it was. Quinn was their leader. Head of a merry band of MMA look-alikes who needed to clear information-sharing through him first. Fine, she'd switch her tactic once they were alone. Hopefully, soon.

"I sensed he was weak before I, uh...returned." Roane flicked his gaze at me. "He was passed out just inside the kitchen entryway."

Britt stood as Roane placed the unconscious man on the couch. "Who is this? Another 'brethren?'" She air-quoted. "And what exactly are brethren? Or am I not allowed to ask that either?"

Possibilities ran through her mind. Were they a part of a secret society? A branch of government kept from the public? They couldn't deny they possessed special skills and weapons. And the ability to take a bullet, several in fact, and still walk upright.

With every second that passed, her chances of getting away from them diminished. She may have been able with just two of them present, but now there were four of them. Remaining outwardly calm was her best hope of lulling them into complacency until an opportunity presented itself.

Britt pushed thoughts of escape away for a moment when the man on the couch, or whatever he and the rest of them were, let out a groan. She may be a prisoner, but her sense of compassion overrode her. Kneeling next to the injured man, she set aside any animosity. After all, over the years, she'd acquired first aid skills in observing medics on her digs, and if she had the ability to help, she would.

She'd officially lost it. Who in their right mind would help the enemy? But this one hadn't kidnapped her, so, for now, she'd use her limited medical knowledge to help. Maybe once awake, this fourth giant would agree to answer her questions.

She checked his vitals and kept an eye on the other three. "What do I need to know about portal sickness, and do you have a med kit I can use?" Her voice shook as she stumbled over the word portal.

Quinn strode over and lifted her up, then placed her a few feet away. He kept a hand tight around her upper arm. "You are not to touch one of my brothers, another Brethren—until the binding ceremony. Your concern is appreciated, but right now, the only thing he needs is rest. His cells require time to heal, and since he's immortal, human medicine doesn't have any effect on him. On any of us."

Her mind buzzed at the word immortal. These men were stone-cold real. Immortal. Deadly. And, oh, my god, they thought she was a fated mate.

"Immortal?" The word squeaked out as she took in a deep breath. Britt tried to break free of his hold. "So, you just slide that into the conversation as if it's nothing?" Her voice shook as she shouted at him.

Quinn squeezed her arm and led her farther away from the other men. To reassure her? To keep her from fleeing? Or to hold her up should she faint from shock. Lord, how was she supposed to react? What did one do or say when you discovered everything you thought to be myth was now to be accepted as fact?

She needed to get away from them as quickly as possible.

She wiggled loose from his grip, intent on retrieving her satchel and making an attempt at the window. Suddenly, a thought slammed into her as she processed their immortality.

Quinn had just been in a firefight with demons. Where was the blood? She whirled on him and poked a finger into his chest. Numerous holes dotted his shirt with little to no blood in them. "You were shot multiple times. Where's all the blood? How could you survive?" She didn't recognize her own voice as she fought to breathe. But she knew the answer.

Frantic, she began to pull on each hole to see beneath the material. Smooth skin greeted her gaze. But that wasn't enough. She tore the front of his shirt until it hung open. Skin exposed from collarbone to navel. No wounds. Not even a goddamn scratch. Just hard-as-steel muscle under smooth-as-silk skin.

Her hands began to shake. "Why aren't you injured?

Who, or what in the hell are you?" Her heart raced. She was drowning, and there was nothing to be done for it. "I saw you get shot. Multiple times."

He grasped her hands and pulled her toward a chair and nudged her to sit down. He forced her head between her knees. Pinpricks of light began to appear behind her lids. Do not pass out, Britt. Immortal. They are all immortal.

"Mac, could you grab her some water, please. No, better make that a shot of whiskey."

"There were bullets. Everywhere. I saw everything. The sides of the car are full of bullet holes... I saw the helicopter implode." With each word, she gulped in air, but it wasn't enough.

"She's going into shock, Quinn. We need to—"

Her head snapped up. "No." She dug deep and fought for control. She'd find the strength—somehow. She was not going to lose it. "I want answers. You promised. Now." In through the nose, out through the mouth. Her breathing eased. Not as choppy as before. She could do this. Immortal or not, she would fight. She would get through this and reclaim her freedom.

"Lass...Britt, you need to eat and have that bath you wanted. There'll be plenty of time for answers soon enough." Quinn's voice held a tinge of panic. Just enough to even her out and provide her with the realization that he wasn't as tough as he portrayed. That maybe he could be bested. Her hysteria had managed to accomplish something positive, at least. It showed her Quinn might just have a weak spot, and she was it.

"Ah, here's Mac and your shot."

She took the glass from Mac, drained its contents, and slammed it on the side table. "Now, Quinn—"

Alarm bells trilled, and for a split second, she thought they were merely in her head—her body's response to the stress. But it wasn't her imagination. Each man jumped into action. Roane picked up Gavin's still form, and Quinn grabbed her and rushed them through a maze of hallways lined with tapestries of battles, and portraits of men—these men, and beasts.

Mac was about ten feet ahead and calling out updates as he led them to an open steel door. A tablet had appeared in his hand. He was scrolling, reading, and running simultaneously.

When Roane, still weighted down by an unconscious Gavin, crossed the room's threshold, the door slammed shut. A series of clicks sounded. The alarms continued to ring out as Mac pulled up a chair to a computer terminal and began keying furiously.

Quinn guided her to a stone conference table and pushed her into a seat. She plugged her ears and looked around the room. Bare of any comfort, the room was meant for business or war. Intricate symbols of swirled and curved lines were painted on the wall above the table. The design was unfamiliar, not anything she'd encountered in her studies. Possibly Egyptian, but there were also indications of Celtic origin. And there was one symbol, an Egyptian Ankh with Celtic swirls that matched the tattoo on Quinn's right arm and shoulder.

Blessed silence filled the room. She scanned the area

to see Quinn sitting at a terminal next to Mac. They were glued to a video feed showing the front of the castle and beyond.

She squinted but couldn't make out anything other than the drawbridge. With just one contact, her vision began to double as she tried to focus. She reached for her bag to retrieve her glasses.

The screen toggled between cameras surveying the entire perimeter of the castle. With her glasses in place, she didn't detect any movement on the screen. Nothing out of the ordinary. Ha! That word no longer applied to her situation.

"Mac, report," Quinn leaned toward Mac's screen.

"The drone is returning as we speak. No signs of a breach. Whatever tripped the sensor is gone."

"Or was never there to begin with."

"Dante?" Roane asked.

"Who else? We haven't had any trouble with the Edinburgh or London cells in months. It must be him. He's the only one with enough power to project the energy required to remotely trip our defenses. And that means he's now aware of our location."

The men shared a look yet avoided eye contact with her.

Britt didn't have to ask why. The battle today and the threat of another rested with her presence. Their hideout had been found. Well, too bad. Not her fault. If they'd left her at the hotel, none of this would be happening. Right about now, she'd be sitting down with her colleagues and celebrating. Instead, she was surrounded by supersized MMA, badass, er... high-lander-esque, men? No, they already told her they were immortal, used portals, and were able to destroy helicopters with a lightsaber George Lucas would envy. They were her doom if she didn't find a way to escape.

As she absorbed her new reality, an inner calm settled in. She now accepted what she'd fought against for years—her ability to sense ancient objects time and time again had nothing to do with luck.

Her father's bedtime stories of the "little goddess-witch" were no fairy tales. She was staring truth in the face, surrounded by immortal beings. The need to finish translating the scroll and figure out the true power of the emerald shard she'd managed to keep a secret had just become her only priority.

Unfortunately, now she'd have to do it while battling demons and denying a soul-deep desire she couldn't shake for Quinn. Dammit, she was so screwed.

CHAPTER
NINE

Quinn wasn't sure how much more physical contact he could take with Britt. She'd freaked out a bit when learning they were immortal, and there was still more to tell her. So much more. Beginning with their other forms, thanks to Mac's slip. She had to suspect something else was different about them.

He and Mac moved away from the consoles and monitors that showed a still empty countryside. The Scottish hare and red deer had bedded down for the night as he wished *they* could. But he knew the quiet was a false sense of security. Demons were on their way. They needed to be gone by morning.

He rubbed his face and thought of the best way to tell her. He needed to be upfront with her, otherwise, the lass may refuse him altogether if he put the truth off. Hell, it'd been less than six hours since he'd taken her from all she knew. How much more truth could the lass handle in one day?

Yet, his inner beast reminded him at every touch of her skin that she belonged to him. It was his duty to tell her everything before she became bound to him. During the skirmish with the demons, he'd barely kept himself from shifting.

It had not been an easy task when his beast had wanted out to play. Coming up with a way to ease his mate into accepting who and what he was would be easier with more time. But that wasn't going to happen.

Now, at the mere thought of shifting, his two-ton, emerald-eyed, and sliver-scaled dragon roared. Quinn clutched the chair in front of him. He glanced down to see claws replacing both thumbs. He released a growled, "Nay, 'tis not time. Behave, or I'll keep you locked up for a fortnight."

His dragon let out a chuff; his thumbs returned to normal. Blessed silence returned. If only dealing with his mate was that easy.

⧌ ⧌ ⧌

"How much do we tell her? What if the binding ceremony doesn't take?" Roane, aka the Rock, asked Quinn as he continued to watch over Gavin.

Britt's ears perked up, but she remained silent. Still coming down from the heart-pumping excitement of racing into an underground bunker, she waited for the men to continue. When seconds turned into a full minute, she opened her eyes in the smallest of slits. Quinn hard turned back to speak with Mac, and Roane was tending Gavin as he began to wake.

Each of the brothers, er...brethren, had long hair except for Roane, and Gavin's was blond. His was full of varying lengths of small braids which were matted to his sweaty head. She'd yet to see him upright, but his size seemed to equal that of Roane's.

Her skin began to itch again, and her stomach rumbled. If they were going to be here a while, she might as well rest up. Closing her eyes, Britt went to her happy place. Images of rolling hills, a cabin by a lake, deer grazing in a meadow, and a comfy outdoor lounger perfect for naps filled her mind. She needed a big reset, but this was the closest she was gonna get.

Time passed, how long she had no clue. When an unsettling hum filled her brain, she opened her eyes to find Quinn a few feet away, staring at her. His face was set in its signature scowl, and his eyes had darkened to a deep green. A swarm of butterflies took flight in her abdomen, and her nipples hardened. Why was he affecting her this way? And now, compared to earlier, he didn't seem to respond to her? For all the fated mate stuff he spouted off earlier, he wasn't acting like one. Instead, he was confusing her.

If he thought a stare down would keep her from finding out the truth, he needed a new strategy. She did her best to ignore the feelings he stirred in her and scanned her surroundings. "What is this room? If you're immortal, couldn't you have used your Spidey senses or something to detect danger?"

Mac chuckled.

Roane reverted to silence.

Gavin, barely awake, coughed.

Quinn continued to stare.

"I like her, Quinn. She can hold her own, and she's funnier than you'll ever be," Mac continued, pounding the keyboard.

"If you won't answer that question, how about this one—"

"What's in your bag, lass? You've had a death grip on it since we arrived."

It was her turn to go silent. She hated being interrupted and Quinn and his merry band of whatever could rot before she gave up the contents of her bag.

Quinn moved closer. "Don't tell me you have the scroll in there instead of under lock and key somewhere."

A bead of sweat rolled down her back. She zeroed in on his full lips and wondered what they would feel like on hers. A real kiss. Without playing pretend for the public. Her brain refused to stop imagining what it would feel like to be caressed and touched in all the right places by him. How much more of this uncontrollable response to him could she handle?

Because kidnapped or not, she'd begun to suspect a small part of her need for him had, in fact, become real.

She held the bag tighter to her chest as he stalked toward her. How had he known about the scroll? Did he also know about the emerald? She had told no one, not even her boss, about her discovery of what she suspected was a part of the mythical emerald tablets. The piece she found was a three-quarter-inch slice of emerald. She'd wrapped it in leather and kept it locked in a reinforced steel box only her thumbprint could open.

If he and the others of his kind knew of the scroll and what it meant to humankind, then would he, would their connection, protect her from the demons?

"Lass?"

She bit her lip to keep herself from responding, from revealing the truth. It would be her bargaining chip, literally, and she would keep it secret until she had no other choice.

"I've reset all the sensors, Quinn. I can't guarantee he won't try again to breach the perimeter, but we'll be ready if he does."

"We need to relocate." Changing course, Quinn opened the steel door.

Britt expelled the breath she'd been holding. She'd been granted a delay. She'd take it.

Quinn held the door for her. "After you."

A dare in his eyes had her rethinking her chances. She almost followed him out. Almost. Britt decided on the spot she wasn't going anywhere. Even as her body ached for him, and the itching had reached a new level of agony, and dammit, yes, she was hungry.

But she wasn't going to give in to his orders.

"No." She sat back down and rubbed her upper arms where the brambles had done their worst.

"No?"

"I'm done with this crap. First, you come clean with the reason why you took me, and don't feed me that bull about fate and some stupid binding ceremony. And second, I want you to take me back to my hotel."

"No." Quinn folded his arms over his massive chest.

"No?"

"You're not the only one who can use that word, lass. You will stay with me. I'm the only one who can keep you and what's in your possession—safe."

"My, someone thinks a lot of himself."

"You have no idea," Mac said.

Quinn raised a hand and waved it toward his brother. Mac let out an "oof" and rubbed his chest. He mumbled something that sounded like "prick" and went back to the computer screen.

She noticed a small tick under Quinn's right eye. He didn't take ribbing well. Good to know.

Time to change tactics. "Is he, this Dantalion, Dante person, demon, whatever, stronger than you?"

"After today's events, I would think it's obvious he's not. At least physically."

Sweet baby Jesus, he answered her without taking one of his long dramatic pauses. Maybe there was hope.

"In strength, I am his superior in every way."

"What aren't you telling me, Quinn?"

"He's a manipulator of minds. He is imbued with the

power to push his thoughts into the minds of men, mortal men. Make them do his bidding. He can make any woman claim her undying love for him with a smile."

Ooh-kay. Not going to put herself in Dante's path. "What does he make them think or do?"

"He commands blind obedience. As what he makes them do? Anything he wants, and the list grows by the day. And...it looks like he wants you."

"Wait a minute. Just hold it right there. How the hell do you know? Maybe he's pissed at you for another reason. Why and how would he know anything about me? I'm just a researcher, a scientist."

"You're so much more than that, and I find it hard to believe you don't know anything about our kind...or yours."

"What? My kind. Okay, now I know you're certifiable. I'm a girl from Nebraska who wanted to dig in the dirt. There's nothing special about me."

"No?"

She hesitated before she answered. "No." Okay, so maybe her father called her "my little goddess-witch," but that was just him being fanciful toward the first girl born in centuries to his line. Right? She had a knack for finding lost objects and later ancient relics when she decided to become an archaeologist.

But she never questioned her heritage. She didn't have time. They moved from place to place, never staying for more than a year in one city or country. When she was ten, her dad had announced she needed to see the world. It was a grand adventure, and she took it for granted. It was something she thought every child experienced.

Britt never knew her mother. She'd taken off when she was a baby. She never thought twice that she had no siblings, no aunts, uncles, or cousins. She never questioned why her dad never remarried, why there were no grandparents, no close friends.

Dammit, Britt, this melancholy is getting you nowhere.

If Quinn wasn't going to give her any more information, Britt would find a way to discover the truth. She'd been alone a long time and knew the only person she could rely on was herself. She'd had to, so putting her trust in others was hard for her.

Could she trust anything Quinn and his brothers had told her? Were they any better than the demons who'd attacked them today?

Discovering the Emerald Tablets had become her life's work. Her obsession. And if Quinn had found out about her ability to locate objects—ancient and magical objects—that meant this Duke of Hell had too.

Time was not on her side.

TEN

"Creator, save me from this stubborn woman." Quinn's hope for a mate had never included a ball-busting beauty. If not for the unmistakable way his body responded to hers and the soul-deep certainty that she was one of the prophesied goddesses, he'd have wished for a more...demure, nay, quiet mate.

But as quick as he processed those thoughts, he banished them. Everything about Dr. Britt Harmony spoke to him and his dragon. Her spicy vanilla scent, her curves meant for the caress of his hands. Her wit and her strength and perseverance in the face of demons and a world unknown to her until now. She was the first of the Brethren's mates, their destiny and the fate of mankind, and he burned to make her his.

"Cat got your tongue, highlander?"

Britt's words brought him back to the moment. He needed to find something for her to do with that sexy mouth of hers other than taking chunks out of his ass. Wrapped around his cock would be a good start. He cursed the image as the mentioned appendage swelled against his fly. Adjusting himself had been unending, and it was only the first day. "Dammit, we don't have time for this, lass. We need to move."

"Wait." A graveled voice echoed off the walls. Gavin pushed himself onto an elbow. His breathing labored.

"Quinn...you need...ceremony...dammit...she needs...protection."

"He's right, Quinn." Roane knelt at Gavin's side and helped him stand.

Quinn raised his face to the ceiling and rubbed his jaw. His brethren came in handy when they were battling demons, but they'd separated centuries ago for reasons beyond watching over mankind more efficiently by each living on a continent. Quite simply, his brothers drove him nuts.

"Gavin, you're in no condition to perform the ceremony. It can wait until you're well enough to follow us."

He turned to Mac, pointing a finger. "If you're not ready in fifteen, we'll go to the portal without you. Roane, see that Gavin is nourished before you leave. Take him to the safe house in Edinburgh until he's ready for another jump. Then let Keir know what's happened."

He swung Britt up in his arms, startling a squeak from her, and strode to his room. Blessedly, she remained silent. However, the closer he came to his room, his concern for her silence changed. A quiet Britt more than likely meant she was plotting her escape.

Convincing her there was no escape from destiny would have to wait until she was safely hidden from Dante.

Quinn turned his thoughts to how to best prepare her for her first trip through a portal. Located on ley lines throughout the world, pockets of space and energy allowed immortals to easily travel from one location to another. Without the benefits of being bound to an immortal and mated, it potentially could be a dangerous attempt for the lass—even with her goddess lineage.

Crossing the threshold, he tossed her onto his bed then opened his weapons closet. He focused on choosing items wisely as they may not be able to return for a while, if ever, and keeping his need for the woman now gracing his room with her tempting scent and mouth on lockdown.

"Hey!" she groaned.

He looked back to see her breasts bouncing as she righted herself on his bed. He suppressed a groan and adjusted himself.

"I could have walked, you know. And you promised me a bath."

"No bath. We don't have time." He grabbed his go bag and focused his attention on locating armor that wouldn't weigh her down. He judged her to be five-eight, one-twenty. She'd need... his bathroom door creaked. He whirled and locked his gaze on her tempting backside as she disappeared.

"Fine. No bath. But I need to use the bathroom," Britt called out. "Wait, do immortals even need to use the bathroom? You're the first one I've met, after all. Oh, this is nice, and you have a rain shower head. I guess you guys do..."

Quinn smirked at her jab, tuned out her chatter, and focused on gathering items she could use to defend herself after their jump.

Precious minutes ticked by, and she'd yet to return. Reaching out with his superior hearing, he picked up the sound of splashing.

"Shite." He dropped the six-inch blade he was contemplating for her, stormed into the bathroom, and stopped short.

Encased in bubbles, she had her eyes closed and hummed a familiar tune he couldn't name. She rubbed her arms with one of his washcloths, droplets forming on her pinkened skin. He cursed as she moved the cloth over the top of her full breasts. A woman had never been in the castle, let alone in his bath.

When he craved a woman beneath him, it was always at a club, in a hotel room, but never here.

"We don't have time for this, lass." He leaned on the doorframe, his hands clenched, knuckles turning white. Pulling her from the tub was not an option. In spite of Gavin's warnings, he knew that waiting to have her under him and begging for her release, and his, until after the binding ceremony was the smart thing to do.

"Get out!"

He ducked as she threw the dripping washcloth; it narrowly missed his head.

Arms crossed over her glistening breasts, she said, "You may not have time, but I made the time. I couldn't take another moment of all that stupid itching. Stupid thorns." She sunk lower into the bath and glared at him.

"Woman, out. Now!"

"Don't call me woman. This is not the Middle Ages or the 1950s, dammit."

He gritted his teeth. "Britt, if you don't get out of that tub, I will drag you out. And I dinna guarantee I won't act on our mutual needs. Because I know you feel the pull as deeply as I do. It's the Fates way of making sure once we've discovered each other, there will be no denying what my Creator, our father, and your goddess ancestor agreed."

She stuck her tongue out at him. "I'm almost done. Just a few more minutes won't mean anything."

Lust slammed into him. He drew in a breath to clear his mind. Big mistake. He took in her unique smell along with the scent of her need. His dragon growled, "Take her now."

Shoving down his beast's demand, he gripped and splintered the door frame. "You have five seconds to decide. Get out on your own or mate with me now. I can't promise you'll enjoy it, but by damn, I'll make you mine, and I'll be yours, and you will submit to our shared destiny."

Britt's mouth dropped open at his words, then slammed shut. Anger bloomed red on her beautiful face.

"You're insane. This whole scenario is crazy. There's not going to be any mating, asshole. I'll be out in a few minutes, and we can discuss you taking me back to my hotel when I'm dressed." She sunk still lower in the bath and gripped the sides of the claw-foot tub.

"It seems I dinna make myself clear enough. We need to leave. Now." He stretched his body to its full height and plucked her from the tub.

She let out a scream that would have busted normal eardrums. He willed himself not to look down; however, he couldn't block out the sensation of her naked, wet skin sliding against his arms and chest. He tried and failed to think of something, anything to keep him from becoming hard, or harder than he'd been since he'd carried her to his room.

He snagged a towel off the shelf as he left the bathroom. "Put this over you." He tossed her onto the bed and turned his back. But he wasn't quick enough. His gaze swept over her full breasts and followed the trail of bubbles along her stomach to the apex of her thighs. He suppressed a groan. Her curves were what he'd always preferred in a woman. Model skinny was not a turn-on for him.

She covered herself just as he caught a glimpse of the triangle of dark curls. He ground his teeth and grabbed the sweats and t-shirt he'd found for her. "Here. Make do with these. We're down to five minutes."

He braced himself for her sharp tongue. Instead, soft whimpers came from his bed. He prayed for strength and looked back at her. She'd wrapped the towel around her upper body, but it only inflamed him more. Her breasts threatened to spill out of the top of the material. Giving comfort was not something he'd ever done. He felt compassion for others, but that was a long way from knowing how to give it.

The best he could do was restrain himself from ordering her to stop crying and put on the clean clothes he'd given her. "Britt, please. We need to go. If you're worried about mating with me, or maybe it's Dante—"

"Dante? Screw Dante. I don't know if he's even real. He's just some bogeyman you've been trying to scare me with. I can handle myself, thank you." She sniffed and rubbed her eyes. "I just need a mini pity party. I'll be fine."

Fine. Yeah, right. Even in his limited experience with human women, he knew the word often meant just the opposite. He watched as she wiggled to the edge of the bed, her towel creeping ever higher on her thighs— *fecking hell.*

"I have had it with your orders. I'll walk back to the hotel if I have to. Now please leave the room so I can dress."

"That was a quick pity party."

She stared at him. He glared back. Her dark-brown hair curled around her shoulders from the steam of the bath and hung down her barely covered breasts. Her toned legs conjured images of being wrapped around his waist.

Shaking his head, he attempted to clear the erotic image. He'd bluffed earlier when he said he'd take her without her wanting him. But he was too mad to correct the declaration he'd force her to submit. That wasn't his style. He wanted her willing and as desperate for him as he was for her.

She stood and flicked her hair back. The regal air about her was enticing. She expected him to follow her command and had yet to back down from him. She was... perfect.

"I'm waiting."

"And you're playing with fire. I'm taller, heavier and I have an arsenal at my feet. I don't take orders well."

"Well, now is as good a time as any to start. I'm serious, Quinn. Hell, I don't even know your last name. Do you have a last name? Doesn't matter; I'm not staying long enough for it to be an issue. I used my cell in the bathroom and called the hotel. They're sending a shuttle to pick me up."

Damn. He'd neglected to take her satchel away from her. "You what?" She had guts, and he wanted her. Now.

"Do I have to repeat myself? It's not my fault you suck at kidnapping. Didn't think to check me for a cell phone, did you?"

He stepped within inches of her. She stepped back. This was a dance he wanted to end in bed, buried deep with her, had it been any other moment in time. Then again, nothing he said or did got through to this woman. Intimidation hadn't worked; maybe seduction would.

"I may not have taken your phone away, but that doesn't mean I didn't think of it." He gentled his words and caressed the side of her face.

"But..."

"But nothing." He moved in closer until she bumped

the edge of the bed and stumbled back, bracing herself on her elbows. He placed a knee next to her hip and leaned over her, swiftly capturing her lips in a soft, gentle kiss. The first taste of her punched him in the gut. The second and third sealed his fate. He wrapped a hand behind her neck and guided her down onto her back. She clutched both of his arms as he continued to take small sips and bites.

Her soft, throaty moan answered his, and he swept his tongue inside and drank his fill. He hadn't expected her reaction to match his desire. He'd hoped for the wildcat but got the willing woman. The quick kiss at the hotel had given him no indication of this.

Someone cleared their throat. He ignored it. Now that he knew what she tasted like, it would never be enough. One kiss was the beginning of the thousands they would share.

"Quinn!" Mac's raised voice filled the room.

Quinn reluctantly broke their kiss, cursing his brother before placing his forehead upon Britt's. Her breathing in rhythm with his. He pulled back to gauge her reaction; her gaze locked on him, smoldering and daring. A sense of triumph flooded him. She was unlike any other woman he'd known. She was...more. And that scared the hell out of him.

Another round of throat clearing rang out.

"What?" Quinn barked.

"Fifteen minutes is up." Mac didn't bother to hide the humor in his voice, then he laughed outright and said, "I'll give you another fifteen. Even though it looks like five will do. I'll be out front."

Quinn pushed himself up off the bed, slammed his door. He cursed Mac's interruption, his own lack of discipline.

No more succumbing to distractions or his naked, almost mate.

"Get dressed, lass. We leave. Now. Unless you want to be captured by a demon and delivered to the Duke of Hell?"

"But the shuttle..."

"Will never arrive. The reason I dinna worry about your cell is simple. Its technology does not work within these walls. A false GPS replaces the actual location of the castle."

"Damn. I don't belong here, Quinn. I choose my destiny, not anyone. Not even the Fates."

"You didn't seem to mind being here when I was kissing you."

He watched as she traced her lips with her fingers, and his cock responded. Creator save him.

"That was a momentary lapse in judgment. Don't worry. Next time I'll make my true feelings known."

He suppressed a grin and tried to block out her mention of a next time. "Dress. We leave in ten."

"In front of you? I don't think so."

"I've already seen all your pretty parts, remember?"

She let out a very loud and unladylike snort and scooped up the oversized clothing, and marched back into the bathroom.

Using world class restraint, he kept his gaze off her retreating form and continued packing up his weapons. Getting her and the scroll safe from Dante was his first priority. Getting her naked again and back into bed would have to wait.

There was no longer any doubt she was his. But he was running out of time, and it was up to him to not freak her out when his dragon form took over as they passed through the portal.

ELEVEN

Britt sighed in frustration. Quinn's words and his devastating kisses enflamed her need for him. Her head and heart battled while she splashed cold water on her face. She patted her face dry, then sighed after loud mumbling drifted under the door. At least she wasn't the only one struggling to make sense of their connection. She stared at her reflection in the oval mirror. Pink cheeks and dilated pupils told her everything she needed to know.

The highlander had her body tied up in knots. It was one of the main reasons she needed to keep her abilities, which he'd indicated he knew of, banked and hidden. Until she was sure of him, of her place in this crazy prophecy turned all too real.

Snippets of her father's fairy tale had already played out since her kidnapping. She'd grown to accept she was different from anyone she'd ever met, but Quinn's declaration of immortality couldn't be true. They had to be mere words. Words meant to scare or reassure her—she hadn't decided which was the truth. But when she did, she had a decision to make.

Follow her destiny or run for her life?

Pushing away from the counter, she reached for the clean clothes. The bath had done its job, and the itching finally stopped, but now she had an all-new annoyance to deal with—clothes nearly five sizes too big. Clothes that carried Quinn's scent. Her body hummed as she pulled the long-sleeved shirt over her head, the hem falling to below her knees. She looked at the pile of ruined clothes in the corner wistfully.

Pulling on the sweatpants he'd given her, the material flopped around her ankles as she moved. She rolled up her sleeves for the fourth time as she reached for the doorknob. At least she was wearing her own shoes.

Quinn stopped stuffing scary-looking knives into a large bag and turned toward her. His gaze lingered over her breasts before traveling down to the floor where the tips of her shoes barely peaked out. "We'll get you better footwear when we arrive at Mac's home." His frown twitched into a grin. "And some clothes. We've never, uh, had a woman in the castle and never thought to stock up on female attire."

No women, ever? She wasn't sure how she felt about that statement as an unwelcome hit of jealousy slammed into her at the thought of Quinn with another woman. Stop it, Britt. The man doesn't owe you fidelity —past or present, just your freedom.

Before she could shake the intimacy of the moment, he tossed her a protein shake.

"You'll need this before we...travel. It won't keep you from feeling ill once we arrive, but it will lessen it." Quinn handed the drink to her, an unreadable expression on his face. He nodded then strode from the room.

She drank the shake and feeling as if she were in a movie, made her way to the main room of the castle to find Quinn and Mac with their heads together. They stopped speaking when they noticed her, and broke apart. Mac picked up his pack, nodded at her, and left.

"Let's go." Quinn guided Britt out the front door and over the bridge. Stepping off the wooden planks onto the dirt path, he dropped his hand from the small of her back.

She brushed off a sudden sense of loss from his touch and stared in awe as Quinn waved a hand toward the castle and strode to the Rover. She was left alone to stare at the ruins she now knew to be a façade.

Had it just been a few hours ago since they'd first arrived? Certainly, days had passed since he stepped in her path and ordered her compliance.

"Lass? Time to go." The men loaded up the nearly destroyed Rover. After the battle, she was surprised it still ran. And now they were off to a location that would transport them magically to where? They were all tight-lipped about it. Although she'd overheard that Gavin had used it earlier, from where was still a mystery. He'd begun to look a bit better, but according to Quinn, he still required further rest from too many "jumps."

What did that mean for her? How would her body react to using a portal? She shivered at the images of being torn limb from limb and forced back a scream at the injustice of her situation.

Her immediate need was to get away from these men. Although she knew her chances of escaping, if she were truly honest, was becoming less and less likely. These men looked like they ate steroids for breakfast, and stood more than a foot taller than she did. She'd need more than mental toughness to overcome their physical strength. And whatever weird, sensual hold Quinn had over her.

"Lass, if I didn't know better, you're ignoring me in the hopes I'll come and get you. That you want my hands back on you." Quinn's tone was low and intimate.

She bit her tongue. Dammit, she had a name, and okay, maybe she wouldn't mind his hands being back on her... Oh, hell. She was determined to keep her thoughts and feelings to herself. The less she said, the less they could guess what her plans were. Once she had plans.

She marched over to the group and watched as they said their goodbyes. Roane would join them after he got Gavin settled into the safe house.

They traveled deeper into the highlands for about an hour before stopping at what looked like a stone circle. Smaller in scale than Stonehenge, the bluestones were about three and a half feet tall. And unlike the famous henge, no green grass filled the inner circle or beyond. It was encompassed by plain dirt and emitted a low hum.

They exited the vehicle and grabbed their gear. She desperately tried to come up with a way out, when a thought hit her. Quinn said her cell phone wouldn't work correctly inside the castle, but now that they were away from it, maybe that meant she could call for help.

She scooted away as slow as she could and faked interest in the landscape. She unbuckled her bag and lifted the flap.

"I'll take that." Quinn's large palm appeared in front of her.

She jumped a foot and landed on one of his boots. "Ow." She hopped away; the sting from the steel-toed footwear radiated up through her leg.

"The phone, lass."

He took her elbow to steady her. His touch ignited goose bumps up and down her arm. She righted herself and sighed. She hadn't heard him approach, dammit. How'd he manage that? She ignored her body's reaction and refused his command. She looked around for...what? Out in the middle of nowhere with four immortal men should have reined in her impossible dream of escaping.

To be honest, and oh, did this hurt, she was becoming tired of the constant standoffs.

"I'm stronger and quicker. Besides, once we pass through the portal, it'll be destroyed. Nothing electronic survives." Quinn held out his hand. The phone vanished.

New questions popped into her head—so much frustration. Control had been taken from her, and she was so tired and on the verge of a tantrum. She'd always been the strong one in any situation. The decision-maker on her digs and research trips. After her father died, she'd grasped on to the one sure thing that would get her through life—control. To have it stripped completely and so suddenly was unacceptable.

"It has all my contacts. Notes, pictures. My life is on that phone, and you want me to willingly give it up?"

His maddening silence had returned.

Please let me keep the phone. Please.

Quinn sighed. "You can't take the cell. We can't afford to have you tracked in any way. But I'll make you a promise that one day you can have it back. When it's safe."

One day. In two words, he summed up her future. One day was all it took to change a life. Her life. Maybe she should tell them what was written on the scroll?

Would he let her go then?

Would he wipe her memory clean as she witnessed him do earlier at the hotel?

More importantly, why hadn't he just done that in the first place and taken her bag? He knew about the scroll she carried. And possibly the piece of emerald.

Why? Unless all of what she learned today was true. That they were immortal, Dante was a real-life demon intent on taking over the world, and she was Quinn's destined mate.

What if she stopped trying to escape and went through the portal and found even greater artifacts than those she'd already found? What if they could explain why she had a sixth sense when it came to the location of lost and mythical relics?

Her head pounded from all the what-ifs. She nodded. "All right. But you promised and one day better be sooner rather than later. Let's get this adventure underway and completed so I can get back to my life."

"Ah, lass. This is your life now."

No. It couldn't be. "Excuse me? Who died and made you God?"

⟁ ⟁ ⟁

THE QUESTION CAUGHT him off guard. One minute Britt was quiet, contemplative, and the next, she's challenging him like no other in his long life had ever dared or lived long after doing so.

His dragon perked up at her words.

Shall we show her now?

Soon, Quinn responded. Because short of binding them together, which now was not the time, getting Britt's cooperation would make their journey much easier.

However, her stubbornness was ruling her at the moment. What he wouldn't give for a bit more time to get her alone. His cock was in a near-constant state of readiness whenever they were close, and he desperately wanted to show her a better way to use her mouth than questioning his every move—a way they'd both enjoy.

"Brother, tell her something, anything, so she'll have a better understanding of what we are and why she's here. We're running out of time." Mac's rushed words reminded them all that Dante's demons could descend at any moment.

Quinn waited a beat before answering. Aye, she deserved the truth. The truth would protect her.

"In a manner of speaking, we are similar to gods. Along with our Creator, we banished your gods. Greek, Roman, Egyptian... all of them."

"What'd they do to piss you off?" Britt laughed.

No one else joined her.

"C'mon, be serious, please? I was only teasing. I mean, you said you're immortal, but you didn't mean it, right? Maybe you've been chemically enhanced somehow. I'm sure the government's figured out how to—"

"You asked, lass. I'm speaking the truth. They played with mankind. Gave them false hope. Used them as slaves."

"Riiight. So... if you're not gods, but you're immortal, that makes you, what?"

"Not from Earth. Well, our father wasn't," Mac answered cheerfully.

An eerie silence followed his declaration. Quinn didn't correct Mac.

"So, your daddy, or whatever you call him, is the OG killer, right?" Britt snickered. "I suppose you all just sprang into existence ready to defend your newly conquered planet? Well, I don't believe a word you've said to me since forcing me from the hotel."

Quinn didn't have time to verbally spar with her. And because so, he found himself disappointed.

She stood up to him as no one else did, and he found it fascinating. He'd find the first opportunity once they were settled to have another match with her. One that ended with them both naked.

"Prepare," he ordered.

"For what? Wait..."

Quinn swept her into his arms and strode inside the henge. For a split second, he wished they'd already gone through the ceremony which would bind them. She'd suffer the effects of the portal sickness less, for one thing. He grimaced at what she was about to experience and brought her body even closer to his.

Shifting into their true form as the Earth's energy swirled around them, Britt's scream was swallowed by the vortex. Her eyes widened in horror as Quinn's face morphed into a long snout, nostrils flared as his dragon took in her scent.

"Mine," it roared.

Quinn's skin vanished, replaced by silver scales, and his hands holding her close became claws. A single flap of his ribbed, razor-sharp tipped wings curled around them as he fully shifted into his dragon. Towering above her as she clutched to his back leg, he rode out the storm, protecting Britt from the intense electric impulses required to move them through space.

His mind filled with prayer to his Creator and, then he added one to the Fates. For a split second, he thought about throwing his mother into the mix before he came to his senses. Because asking for help from Athena was the last thing the Brethren needed.

And he didn't need his brothers on his case about bringing their mother back into their lives—prophecy, or no prophecy.

TWELVE

Quinn shifted back into human form as Britt's piercing screams threatened to rupture his eardrums. To be fair, he'd neglected to tell her to keep her eyes closed until they'd arrived at their destination. He'd hope to ease her into the reveal of his other half and now acknowledged that failure.

He wouldn't be so shortsighted in the future. Her wellbeing, physical and mental, were his top priority.

He willed away his dragon's disappointment, and shifted back into his human form. Naked and fighting the energy waves pummeling all around them, he lifted a hand, his clothing returned as Britt was momentarily unsupported between Quinn's next breath and his curse that followed. A swirl of indigo, violet, and white slashes of light carried them along the ancient ley line to their destination.

Extending an arm to secure a now unconscious Britt,

he failed to reach her in time as the vortex expelled them. Landing on his hands and knees, supplication was the price paid for traveling in human form through any portal. He gasped in a lungful of dry, hot air, his chest expanding till it threatened to burst from the pressure change.

Britt lay prone to his left, and for a moment, he feared her dead. The first trip through the portal was the worst by far for any immortal but doubly so for fragile humans. He sat back on his haunches, leaned over, and swung her into his embrace. Scanning her still, small form, he took note of her shallow breaths and thanked the Creator for keeping her safe.

Remorse overtook Quinn as he wished he could have spared her that first glimpse of his dragon. He'd never had to show his other half to anyone not of his kind before, and it was that neglect that would now haunt him. His only solace was that once bonded, her future trips would be less painful.

"Oh, *mo chridhe*. Please wake," he whispered his plea, his deep brogue thick and raspy. Developing a tolerance to portal travel took time, and he feared she might be out for a while.

He scooped her into his arms, stood and searched for Mac.

Britt stirred and let out a gasp. Relieved, he looked down at her wide-eyed expression, her hair tangled about her face as she gulped in fresh air. It boded well that she could handle the stress on her system from the often-unforgivable vortex.

The sound of his name snapped his attention to the west of them. Mac appeared over a slight rise in the distance, jogged over to their position, his aviators firmly in place against the ruthless late-summer sun. Temperatures in the desert reached well beyond a hundred, and that was on a cool day.

"What is this place?" Britt choked out, her voice thin and weak.

"We're in Central America. Our secure location is fifty miles away. But first, we need to stop in the closest town, secure our transportation and load up on supplies."

Britt's breathing had normalized, and she pushed against his chest. Quinn narrowed in on her movements, his gaze locking with hers.

"Put me down." Her plea came through gritted teeth.

The portal hadn't taken away her fighting spirit, and for that, he was not only grateful but he felt a strange sense of pride in his intended mate.

Ignoring her, he worried she'd succumb to the heat if he didn't find her appropriate clothing soon. He doubted she'd strip to her bra and panties to trek through the desert. The image brought a smile to his lips and an ill-timed surge of lust.

With great restraint, Quinn set her down gently and rummaged in the closest bag till he found and handed her a bottle of water. "Down this. We need to be on our way and out of the direct sun."

Britt looked at his go bag with a hopeful look on her face.

"So, that's it? We're not talking about what just happened?"

That's precisely what he intended. "You need a hat."

Frowning at his lack of forethought, he rummaged in his pack and found a small towel. That would have to do. Dousing the fabric with water, he placed it over her head. The makeshift hat did nothing to dispel her beauty. She could be dressed in rags, and he'd still want her. A want that was quickly growing into need. Quinn adjusted himself as she began drinking.

He watched in fascination as Britt tipped back her head, her neck glistening with escaping droplets of water as she drained it dry. A low groan escaped his lips. Her gaze snapped to his face. Quinn covered his response with a coughed, "How are you feeling?"

She tossed the now empty bottle to him and placed her fists on her hips. "Other than nauseous, a headache for the ages and sweat pouring out of me—everywhere —I'm just peachy? And you?"

Damn, she was cute when she was grumpy.

"Why are you grinning at me? It's blazing out here, and I'm about ready to strip. I would kill for a tank and shorts right now. And an explanation for what I saw."

He sucked in a deep breath. "No killing necessary. And thanks for the visual by the way." If Mac wasn't with them, he'd insist she strip. Dammit, did she not have an idea of what she was doing to him?

"There's a town about five miles north of here. We'll get you some cooler clothing and stock up on provisions. Trace keeps an ATV stored there for emergencies. It'll be another forty plus miles from there to our—"

"Fine. Ignore me. But this isn't over, highlander. You will tell me what I saw in the portal, and... wait, we still need to go somewhere else? What's the good of using a portal if we still need to travel to your secret hideout?"

Quinn rubbed his jaw to keep from taking the bait. Dealing with an angry woman was something new, yet fascinating. He began to wonder if she was as passionate in bed as she was in this moment. He was looking forward to finding out.

"Oh, I know, why don't you just wave your hand as you did with the castle and 'poof,' the super-secret hideout is right next to the unexplainable rift in the Earth's atmosphere."

Mac began chuckling. "Great question. It seems, uh, an unexpected shift occurred this time 'round. Typically, we're spit out a heck of a lot closer."

Quinn marveled at her resilience, but they were losing daylight and needed to be on their way. "Lass, going 'poof' isn't exactly as easy as it looks. There needs to be a structure already in place, and besides, if you take another look around, we're at an ancient site where typically, tourists are crawling around, every day of the week. We just got lucky that the park is now closed. No witnesses.

"Now, I need you to do exactly as I say so we make it to our destination—safely, before dark. Keep up on your water intake. Be sure to tell either Mac or me if you need a break. Understood?"

She nodded. The fight, it seemed, had been sucked out of her by the intense heat in the short amount of time since their arrival. Her paleness worried Quinn. But he wasn't going to press his luck; they needed to leave. He tossed her another water bottle and loaded up his pack, and began walking.

He'd taken only half a dozen steps when from behind him, he heard Britt yell.

"Wait, this is Chichén Itzá? Oh, my god... I've always wanted to come here. Can't we take some time to—"

"No."

"But it's fricking Chichén Itzá. This is...wait...I'm sensing..." Britt's voice faded and she stopped walking.

He ground his teeth together. "Britt, there is no time. Let's go." Quinn continued on, not bothering to turn and make sure she followed.

"Uh, Quinn. Something's up with Britt. Look." Mac was standing a few yards behind them. He nodded toward Britt, concern lacing his features.

Quinn gazed between his brother and his mate. Mac shrugged his shoulders and gazed back at the pyramid Britt's focus was centered upon.

"It's too soon for her to succumb to the heat, right?" Mac asked.

"Aye." Quinn covered the distance between himself and Britt. "Lass, another day. We'll return and you can spend all day exploring." He reached out and placed a hand on her shoulder.

Britt jumped at the contact. She shook her head and

glanced up at him. For a moment her eyes were clouded, then cleared. She nodded. "Um, yeah, fine. Another day."

Unsure what he'd witnessed, Quinn motioned for Mac to take the lead and waited for her to begin walking. When she passed him, he could have sworn he heard a mumbled "asshole" under her breath. Yeah, he could be one of those on occasion, but right now, he was the boss. And what he said goes.

Two miles in, a heaviness descended around them, and the air changed. Each breath became a struggle. Something dark and sinister had entered the area. He shouted at Mac, "You feel that?"

Mac nodded and searched the area behind them. "I'm not seeing anything out of place."

Quinn closed his eyes and scanned the landscape for additional life forms. He sensed several lizards, innumerable insects, and a demon—a demon not allowed by treaty to leave the realm buried beneath the human one.

Upon opening his eyes, Quinn sighted the Duke of Hell a hundred yards away. The demon's image flickered. The figure moved closer to them and disappeared only to reappear seconds later.

Closer.

Another flicker interrupted his foe's image, and the truth of the situation became clear.

The Duke of Hell had a new trick.

CHAPTER
THIRTEEN

uinn squinted against the sun's glare and refocused his gaze on Dante. The demon was dressed in a shiny gray Italian suit. Pale skin in sharp contrast to his dark hair slicked back between ebony horns and his midnight gaze locked on Britt.

Trembling at Quinn's side, Britt placed a hand on his arm. Her nails were digging into his biceps, leaving tiny divot marks. She pressed her face into him and shuddered. Quinn's body vibrated in response to her fear.

Mine, rang out in his mind. *Protect*, demanded his dragon.

Battle ready, he placed his hand on the hilt of his sword, withdrawing and raising it above their heads. It rang out a high-pitched song, glowing green as Quinn compelled it to encompass the three of them in an energy shield separating them from any attack by the demon.

He didn't know what to expect from this projection of Dante, but he would be damned if the demon took another step toward them. The shield would cost him physically, but it was worth it to keep Britt safe.

"So, is this him? The Duke of Hell, Dantalion?" Britt's voice was soft yet steady and strong.

He leaned down to reassure her. "Lass, it's merely an image of him. He's not corporeal, and yes, he's the one who ordered the attack on us today, then tripped the perimeter alarm at the castle."

"How do you know that for sure?"

"Trust me. It was him." Quinn would bet his stock portfolio the Duke of Hell had come for his mate.

"Is he stronger than you?"

Quinn paused before he answered. It was complicated. "If I answer yes, are you going to try and escape and go to him for help?"

"Trade one kidnapper for another? I hardly think so. But he looks familiar. Like I've seen him somewhere before."

"No," Quinn responded to her question of his strength versus the demon's, and pushed back the thought that she had seen Dante before today. He'd worry about her troubling statement later.

"No, what?"

"We are equal in our power; however, we each possess special objects which make our battles—interesting."

"Your sword?" Britt's gaze landed on the object in his hand.

"Aye."

"And his... what's his weapon?"

"As I explained earlier, it's his mind." Quinn ground out the words. It was the one weapon Quinn had yet to find a way to block entirely.

"Well, I didn't believe you—then."

He ignored her and continued. "Any thought he has can be pushed inside the mind of a mortal. He can make any woman cry out in despair—or desire—for him."

"And for a man?"

"Despair. Anger. Blind obedience."

She shivered at his words. "My head hurts. It's as if... as if he's digging into my forehead, the pressure. It's awful."

Getting her to safety and far away from the mind-bending demon couldn't happen fast enough. The Brethren had been battling the demon race for centuries; this duke was one of many who had tried to find a way to take over humanity. Quinn had seen firsthand the madness created by Dante and his fellow monsters. Psychopaths and Satan worshippers amongst the humans were nothing new; however, numbers had increased, and keeping the mortals from succumbing to the underworld had become the Brethren's greatest concern—now more than at any point in their long existence.

And now it appeared Dante was after his fated mate.

Quinn, and his brethren's entire existence, was their sire's attempts to protect humanity against itself and the underworld. It was nothing less than pure arrogance and inflated ego, but their father had seen a need when he'd become stranded on Earth and used his otherworldly powers to carry man beyond the Bronze Age.

Shaking off his daddy issues, he looked down at Britt's tired and weary but always gorgeous features. The pull he felt toward her continued to grow; his body's demand to make her his would soon overpower his every waking moment. Getting her to safety and conducting the binding ceremony was now more urgent than ever.

"Don't let his handsome outward appearance fool you, lass. He may look like a movie star, but he's a monster. Through and through."

"Speaking of monsters, let's get back to when we were in the portal, I... I thought I saw ... that you became something that surely must have been a trick of the mind. But, Quinn, I swear I saw scales appear on your skin and—"

Quinn gently gripped her upper arms and turned her to face him, his eyes locking on hers. "I am nothing like him. I am your mate. You. Are. Mine."

"You didn't seem very happy about that before. Why the change of heart now?"

"I... I have trouble with authority, but I protect what's mine. And till this moment, I didn't have anything to compare my feelings to. Now I do. You are mine, Britt. Whether you want it to be so or not."

A blast of vicious, negative energy enveloped them. Quinn tore his gaze from the fear in Britt's eyes and faced the evil being he would do everything in his power to destroy.

"Telling tales, dragon? *Tsk, tsk.* However, I will let it pass as you have been so good as to find my beloved."

Quinn pushed Britt behind him, shielding her. "She is mine. And you will never touch her, demon." He surprised himself with the intensity of the snarled words. He had long thought it would be his decision to accept his chosen mate or not. The Fates were surely having a good laugh at his expense somewhere in the heavens.

"I had despaired of ever having her. And here she is. Don't worry, my love. I've sent my best soldiers to collect you." Dante's voice breached the energy shield.

Quinn's dragon screamed. Pain burst inside his skull. For a brief moment, as he watched Dante's features form a grotesque smile, Quinn saw the demon's true form. Britt showed no reaction to the flash of change, however.

"Britt, my love. Soon we'll be together. Whatever this *man...* what are you calling yourself now? Oh, yes, *Quinn.* Whatever Quinn has told you, it's false. I'm your destiny. Hold on for me. Your ancestor promised you to me, Britt, with her dying breath. You are my goddess."

"What is he talking about, Quinn?" Her voice was small and tearful.

The fear in her voice almost undid Quinn.

"Ah, I see you're confused. No one told you of your heritage? No? Well, there's time for that when we're finally together, and your true powers are unleashed."

Dante's smile widened. "Come to me, my love. Yes, that's it. Fight the dragon. We belong together."

Quinn bore down to deflect Dante's hold over Britt as he strengthened the shield. Sweat poured off him as veins pulsed and muscles bulged, his mind and body fighting his dragon's need to shift and attack.

If he shifted now, Britt would be injured and possibly killed within the protection of the energy sphere as the shift would outpace the magical barrier, severing their protection.

"Resist the pull, lass. I'm not sure how his words will affect you as he's not here in the flesh. Block his thoughts."

Quinn held his mate tighter as she began to struggle out of his arms under Dante's thrall. The demon's sultry voice weaved a snake charmer's chant toward Britt.

"Lass, his words hold no truth. It's all lies. You are a daughter of Brigid, Goddess of Life. Push him out of your mind."

Britt nodded and squeezed her eyes closed at his plea. Her shaking concerned him. She was not yet strong enough to defeat Dante's compulsion. Not without the binding ceremony's power that would unleash her magic and give her immortality. Feeling a desperation foreign to him, Quinn grasped tighter onto Britt's arms and swore at the blooming bruises his strength created on her delicate skin.

Britt leaned ever closer in Dante's direction as the barrier around them began to shimmer and thin. "Yes, my liege, I understand. I am yours," she said, her voice monotone.

The devotion he heard in her whispered words stole Quinn's breath. He turned his attention to Dante, who had ceased to speak, the demon's eyes now red and glowing. There was no doubt he was compelling Britt's gaze to remain on him and communicating with her telepathically.

Out of time, Quinn released one of Britt's arms, raised his now free hand and called forth the unused energy from their trip through the portal, and sent a pulse aimed at Dante.

Sparks emanated from Quinn's fingertips, narrowing into a thin ethereal green line wrapping around the Duke of Hell's astral form. Quinn roared, "Begone!"

A clap of thunder rang out. A blinding explosion of light filled the space between them, immediately followed by eerie, complete silence.

FOURTEEN

Britt felt more than heard Quinn's shout of "fucking bastard" as he returned his sword to its sheath. All senses on overload, she gulped air and took several long, deep breaths.

With the demon's voice still ringing in her ears, she coughed from the taste of sulfur, its stench still hanging in the air. Squinting, she caught sight of the last sparks of energy as they winked out. Her skin erupted in a cold sweat, and she shivered, then rubbed her arms, desperate to rid the slimy film Dante's final words had created. *That was just a nip, my love. A taste of what it will be like between us. Soon, I will be with you in the flesh, and I will destroy these Brethren for you. For daring to hide you from me. Don't let him touch you, Britt. There will be consequences if you do. You're mine.*

She craned her head to look at Quinn. "Why? Why me?" she whispered.

He crouched next to her. In comfort? No, that

couldn't be right. The man she'd come to know in such a short time didn't know how to comfort, only command. He was just making sure she didn't crack after what happened. She needed to toughen up if she was going to survive this ordeal.

Romanticizing the situation would be ludicrous. Accepting Quinn's choices meant trusting him, and trust was something she had in short supply. There was no one she could trust and hadn't been in well over a decade.

Quinn's drawn-out silence and soul-piercing stare left her more confused than ever. Shouldn't he want her to know everything? Know the reasons for Dante's words and his appearance, albeit remotely, from freaking hell. What was so damn special about her?

Well, screw the highlander's stoicism. "He was in my head. He was describing filthy things and telling me how much I'd crave his touch—not yours. And oh my god. He knows things about me. About my father—how he was killed. And my private thoughts. He said I was his, Quinn. That your claim over me is false. Who do I believe? Tell me."

Quinn stood and took two long strides away from her. Britt's gaze traveled down his large form, broad shoulders, narrow waist, and firm backside. Ugh. She should be furious with him for keeping her in the dark, not drooling over the man who, to this point, had been less than forthcoming.

He turned and set his stance, his legs spread wide, hands on hips. "I wish things had gone differently, lass.

All of it. From the moment we met earlier to now. If I could I—"

"What? What would you do differently, because we didn't just meet, did we? You kidnapped me. Took me from my life and thrust me into this never-never land world with demons, immortals, and...and dragons. A dragon, Quinn. You. Tell me it wasn't—I dare you because that's what I saw in the portal. And that's what the freaking duke of the underworld called you." Her body shook, and her mouth had gone dry. She reached into the bag for another bottle of water, opened it with shaking hands and waited.

She peeked at his face for a reaction as she took a deep drink. She wanted something, anything from him to make her feel less crazy, less alone. Instead, he pursed his lips and looked away.

Britt continued to stare at him. It was as if the gods had created him and Quinn's chiseled profile intrigued her. But his prominent cheekbones and his silver hair didn't exactly scream Scottish heritage. So what was he, really? Hell, nothing about him, the Brethren, Dante, none of it made sense. Her head continued to pound as she attempted to work it all out.

Turning away from him, she finished her water, then glanced back as if an invisible force couldn't stand her attention not being on him. She groaned in frustration. Fated mates, destiny, and her body's growing need for Quinn were becoming overwhelming.

First, she needed to find out if the demon would be back anytime soon. And if so, could Dante's ability to remotely project himself hurt her? She was a scientist, dammit; she should be able to make sense of it all. But this? This person or whatever "it" was, had touched her mind, her soul, and he'd been merely projecting his image. What would happen once he was in her presence—actual flesh and blood. Did demons have blood?

And Dante had called Quinn "dragon." That couldn't have been a coincidence. What she witnessed in the portal had been real. And now dragons, immortal men and demons were a part of her world, and Quinn was stonewalling her.

Dropping to the ground, she hugged her knees to her chest. She turned her head toward a hushed conversation and noticed Quinn and Mac with their heads together. Probably deciding on what secrets to share with her. Or maybe making up a story to keep her from bolting.

The memory slammed into her. A childhood fairy tale broke free and whispered to her. A young girl with glossy dark hair to her waist wearing a loose and flowing gown of white with gold thread weaved throughout. A colorful bird followed her everywhere, frequently gifting her with shiny and sometimes strange objects.

She'd thought her father a genius storyteller, a fearless adventurer, and the kindest person she'd ever known. Then he was violently taken from her. The last night they'd been together, he'd added a new chapter to her favorite tale of the young girl with powers beyond comprehension.

Britt had loved her father and his stories full of adventure while serving others. He'd been big on that during his short life as well. The princess had been chosen to protect Earth, keeping it free of creatures from the underworld. And her future children would...would what? Pieces of the story were still missing. No matter how hard she'd tried to recreate them over the years, details remained elusive.

Today's events, as fantastical as they were, had been eerily familiar.

Her father had called the young girl Brigid, and she was a princess, not a goddess. Hadn't she heard Quinn call her that as Dante attempted to take over her free will?

In the story, Brigid was labeled a witch by the frightened townspeople and often located lost items in trade for a meal and a warm place to stay on her travels. Was Britt's uncanny ability to locate ancient objects based on witchcraft? It was a question she asked herself often, yet refused to pursue. It was a path she hadn't wanted to pursue. Perhaps she should have.

"You ready, lass?" Quinn returned, yet remained at a distance.

"Is he the devil? Satan?" Why she needed to know, Britt couldn't say, but she felt it in her bones that it mattered, somehow.

"No, lass. Worse."

"What's worse than those things?"

Quinn held out his hand. "He wants to be those things and more. And if you're thinking of running from me, to him, know that I will do everything in my power to find you, keep you safe. And then after we're officially bound, and we've had time to enjoy each other, I promise no more secrets between us. You have my word. You belong at my side, lass."

Dammit. The words "enjoy each other," while mild, produced wicked images of them together. Could she put her trust, her life, in someone else's hands? Someone who'd kidnapped her yet stirred her desires, who created needs so intense, she was ready to pounce on him even now. Could she share her truth with Quinn and be bound to him no matter the cost?

There were too many unanswered questions. She could not, would not allow herself to follow—anyone—blindly. So, first things first.

Britt threw her shoulders back. "Show me your true form, and you have my word I'll not run." The words left her in a rush before she thought them through, all without taking a breath. She closed her eyes and silently counted to twenty.

FIFTEEN

"Open your eyes, lass." Quinn let loose a heavy sigh. As much as Britt wished it of him, there was no time for show and tell. He motioned over to Mac. "Contact Trace. Let him know we'll be arriving by nightfall."

He kept his gaze on Britt's upturned face, noting her full lips and stubborn chin. His blood ran hot at all the places where he wanted her mouth to explore. If she didn't respond soon, he was on the verge of breaking his vow to keep his hands off her until they wed.

Britt's eyes flashed open. Her disappointment immediate. Her eye roll drew his attention to her imperfectly perfect pupil, and the truth of their circumstances slammed into him.

The Goddess Brigid had bestowed gifts upon Britt and all the others yet to be found. And it ignited his need to make her fully his. He knew he was on borrowed time, but getting her to safety had to take precedence.

"I'm willin' to share just one thing before we go through the binding ceremony, lass. Each of us, the Brethren, are not only brothers, but keepers of the sacred Emerald Tablets. And each of us has an alternate and different form, gifted by our mother when we were born. The rest of our story, my story, will be transferred to you in an instant after we are bound to one another."

"So, you're not all dragons. Good to know. And that was more than one thing. Thanks for the vague-splaining." Britt stomped off toward her satchel, snatched it up, securing it crosswise on her body, all the while keeping her back to him.

"What the hell is vague-splaining?" Quinn threw up his hands.

"Quinn!" Mac shouted.

"Not. Now." He ignored Mac and focused on her. It was fast becoming all about her.

Britt whirled to face him, sending her hair flying. Damn, she was something when she was pissed.

"I just made it up. Stop treating me like I don't have a right to know... you... you—dragon! I need—"

A crack of thunder rang out, shocking Britt into silence. The smell of ozone descended upon them.

Britt screamed, Mac snorted, and Quinn groaned. "Fuck me."

Fate had dropped in. Literally.

One of the Fates, anyway. The craziest one.

Quinn made sure he stood between Britt and Clotho. This Fate may not have the power to end their lives, but she directed everything between birth and death—reason enough to stay on her good side.

"This is not going according to plan. No, no, no. Not one bit." The deity paced, her long silver robe dragging behind her, kicking up dirt that shouldn't be there.

"Clotho, to what do we owe this...unheard of honor?" Quinn shifted his body, mirroring the Fate's movements, protecting Britt. Where were her sisters?

She was rumored to be the firstborn of Zeus and Themis, and it was said she, Lachesis, who determined length of life, and Atropos, who cut the cord, determining a person's death, were more powerful than their father. Today was not the day Quinn wanted to test that theory.

"Why have you two not copulated?" Clotho stopped. Her eyes glowing, she zeroed in on Quinn.

A strangled snort-cough erupted from behind him. Quinn lifted his arms to keep Britt in place. "She's one of the Fates, lass. Watch your tone." He whispered the plea only loud enough for Britt's ears—hopefully.

Mac approached them slowly and stopped, coming even with Quinn's left shoulder. "Do we bow, or what?"

The Fate let out a high-pitched cackle. "You, I like. And when your time comes to be with your chosen mate, I have no doubt you'll perform your duty timely. It's already been written, Mackenzie, and I have the perfect one for you, but not now. The time is not quite right."

Mac's back went ramrod straight, and his lips thinned until they almost disappeared. Quinn knew what his brother was feeling. Being told you had no choice in your mate and your duty was to knock her up immediately had made all of them bitter toward the Fates. Some more than others.

For him, it made the compulsion to bed Britt no less enjoyable, since he was confident after spending time with her, he'd want her regardless of destiny, but it was still a hard pill to swallow.

In less than a blink, Clotho stood toe to toe with Quinn. "You, my boy, are just like your sire. Well, as close to him as any of you are save for Gavin. He was...reluctant to mate your mother, at first. Then there was the Zeus problem. But he soon learned we do things differently than where he'd come from. So, perhaps I didn't account for the otherworldly stubbornness within you. No matter. See it done by the third dawn. If the Brethren are to succeed against that idiot Duke and the others, then your numbers need to increase."

Another strangled sound came from Britt as she maneuvered around Quinn. He wrapped his arm around her waist and held her tight to his side, her feet dangling several inches above the ground.

"Let me go. I have a say. Wait, don't go!" Sweaty and pissed, Britt struggled against his tight hold as the Fate vanished.

Letting out a sob, Britt continued to squirm. "Is nothing negotiable in your world?"

He released her even as his body, his dragon, protested. Clotho's reminder doubled his need to "copulate" with Britt. He gazed down into her tear-filled eyes, wishing he had the right words to banish her anguish, instead of the truth she needed.

"This is *your* world, lass. It always has been."

Britt pushed away from him, and for the first time in his very long life, he understood what the humans referred to as heartache.

"I don't know whether to kiss you or punch you. I'm so..." Britt marched off, cursing fate, prophecy, and someone named Greg.

Quinn watched as she stood, staring at the ancient temple, her hands taming her hair into a ponytail before she wrapped her arms around her middle. He hadn't wanted to tell Britt the real reason they were experiencing such intense sexual desire between them. He'd wanted some control over the where and the when, but now, even that had been taken from him. Could this day get any worse?

Mac cleared his throat. "I hate to pile on, but Trace isn't responding."

SIXTEEN

"What the—" Britt pushed hair off her face and scrambled to her knees in the middle of one of the largest beds she'd ever seen.

"You passed out right after Clotho left. I'm surprised you made it through the portal. Most humans are out for hours. So, I carried you to El Castillo, then we grabbed Trace's truck and arrived here while you still slept." Quinn pushed off the doorframe. "Mac and I are working on where our brother took off to. The supplies we picked up last night are on the counter in the kitchen."

Britt stared open-mouthed at the arrogant high-lander's perfect ass as he left her to figure out exactly where the hell here is.

And she needed caffeine—desperately. But she caught a whiff of herself and decided a shower took precedence. Embarrassment overcame her, and she hoped Quinn hadn't noticed.

She changed into clothes she found in the dresser. Quinn must have picked up a few things while she was unconscious. The sizes were close, but the style was...not her. She favored archeology chic: wrinkle-resistant chinos, loose-fitting neutral-colored blouses, and broken-in Timberlines. The cotton shorts and sleeveless, bright-pink blouse would have to do. At least they'd be cool.

Her stomach rumbled. When was the last time she'd eaten? It had to have been at least twenty-four hours since she'd had a pot of coffee and a cinnamon bun before her lecture... her career-making, dig-funding speech that never happened. Britt double-checked the contents of her bag and went in search of something to eat.

So much had occurred since yesterday morning, and now she was in a house that was an eclectic mix of adobe neutrals and modern tech. Smart-home display panels mounted on every wall. The thought of walking out the front door crossed her mind. But then what? She needed to be shrewd about escaping from a secure home, far away from the Duke of Hell, and out into a country she knew little about.

The house looked to be one level until she passed a set of stairs going down. She heard the murmur of voices, Quinn and Mac's, she hoped. Her stomach protested again. Deciding food and coffee were her priorities, she continued through a large room furnished with ultra-modern chrome tables and leather chairs. A flat-screen TV at least sixty inches hung above a glass-fronted fireplace opposite floor-to-ceiling windows overlooking the desert.

She remembered Quinn saying this was her world now shortly before she passed out. If it was, she needed to figure out the best way to navigate it, and she needed more information about the prophecy and her supposed role in it before she took off. Because the longer she was with Quinn, the more chance there was she would succumb to the need to jump his bones, and if that happened... there would be no going back to her life. Maybe.

Also, she couldn't shake the claim by Dante that she was a witch. The claim was too close to that of one of her father's favorite nicknames for her: little goddess-witch.

She knew the gift she possessed was unexplainable at best. Still, the ramifications of losing what she'd discovered to anyone, even the self-proclaimed Brethren, could become her worst nightmare come true. Britt quickly realized that her father hadn't prepared her properly for what her power meant to the world, despite the many fairy tales he told her. They began to bounce around in her head until it started to ache.

Chocolate. And coffee. Britt would kill for some chocolate right about now.

Britt entered the kitchen and rummaged through the cupboards. No chocolate. Not even a piece of hard candy. But she did find coffee and began measuring grounds, filled the water tank on the fancy machine, and waited. She'd been running on adrenaline and hope for hours. Not a combination she was used to.

Spying grocery bags, she found only canned goods and snacks. Turning to the enormous double-sized refrigerator, Britt began pulling out eggs, juice, and started humming. She found a skillet and located a loaf of bread.

"Lass, I was hoping you'd find your way here." Quinn walked into the kitchen.

She looked and found him smiling at her. His grin gave her pause. Seriously? *This* is what got him to smile.

"What is it with men getting off on seeing a woman working in the kitchen?"

He shrugged and leaned against the counter. He crossed his feet and braced his arms behind him on the edge of the granite. Britt wondered which was stronger. The stone or the man? She locked on his rock-hard arms and sighed—definitely the man.

"It's always a turn-on to see a woman take care of you." He poured himself a cup of coffee and kept his gaze locked on hers as he sipped.

"Hey, I haven't had my first cup yet." She pushed him aside and filled her cup, and searched for the creamer.

"And I'm not taking care of you. I'm hungry." His stare made her nervous. A feeling she rarely experienced around men. "So, tell me this, if I paraded around in a bikini or lingerie, you wouldn't be as turned-on as you are at this moment because, in your mind, I'm taking care of you?"

"It's more than the skin on display. At least for me.

Physical attraction doesn't always have to be so blatant."

"I call bullshit. I've yet to run into a man who would take a home-cooked meal over a sure thing." Britt set her coffee on the island between them. Her fingers itched, and her nipples hardened at his closeness. As hungry as she was for breakfast, her body was demanding more than food.

"I guess you've been around the wrong men."

"And you're the right one?" Britt snickered.

"Apparently."

She watched as a flush crept up his neck and settled on his high cheekbones. He was silent so long, she wasn't sure he would add anything else to his answer. But she really wanted him to. A life-or-death wanting. And suddenly Images of them rolling around in that big bed made her achy.

"If I say please, will you make enough food for all of us?" Quinn flashed her a blinding smile.

She sighed at her weakness for men with killer smiles. "What would you like with your eggs? I might as well cook for you since I've already got everything out, but don't get used to this. I'm no cook. I can do the basics, and that's about it." Turning back to the counter behind her, she began to crack eggs into a bowl.

"I'll get some steaks out. Mac should be up soon. He's attempting to find Trace's last known coordinates via his call to us a couple of days ago. We thought he was here; we were wrong."

His voice had changed and deepened as he spoke of

his missing brother. They all obviously cared for one another, and it hit her square in the abdomen, igniting butterflies.

Now is not the time to get all gooey and soft, Britt.

Quinn opened the fridge and removed a large package wrapped in butcher paper. His smile had turned into more of a grin, and his gaze captured hers. His eyes had turned a darker green as he swept her from head to toe. The lingering attention he paid to her breasts had her holding her breath until he zeroed in on her face. His gaze sobered as he held out the steaks to her.

Britt cleared her throat. "Dinner for breakfast, huh? Okay, I can handle that." She took the package, unwrapped them and put them under the broiler, then quickly put some distance between them.

"I didn't see any vegetables in the supplies, so scrambled eggs or..." She fought the urge to look over her shoulder. He was still close; by the sound of his movements, probably right next to the island, finishing his coffee.

"Eggs are fine, no vegetables. All we need is protein. Everything else is just filler."

"No vegetables? Lucky kid. One less thing for your mom to cook, huh? My dad was always trying to trick me into eating my veggies."

"I didn't have a mom. Well, not a normal mom. We had a... female who gave birth to us, but we were given to a caregiver to raise us, and... that's a part of our past better left for another time."

"No mother? Wow, I didn't think we would have

anything in common." Britt paused. A need to comfort him overwhelmed and confused her. Quinn was quickly worming his way into her heart, and that couldn't happen if her not-yet-formulated escape plan had a chance at succeeding. "I didn't have one either. I mean, mine took off right after I was born, so it was just my father and me."

She waited for him to say something about their similar start in life, but he turned away and began to set the table in the corner of the kitchen. Shrugging her shoulders, Britt turned back to preparing their meal.

Ten minutes of awkward silence later, she removed the steaks, then set them aside to rest. She cracked half a dozen eggs into a skillet and tended them in between long sips of coffee. Sighing, she was finally beginning to feel halfway normal.

When the food was ready, she handed him his plate, and their fingers brushed. A wave of yearning overcame her, causing her to sway.

Off-balance, she locked her knees to keep from falling and took in a deep breath to calm herself. Instead of fresh air, she breathed in Quinn's unique scent. It had the uncanny effect of calming her, yet triggered her libido at the same time. This was not the time to be imagining him kissing dend touching her, bringing her to the edge of orgasm as his nimble fingers worked her wet folds and... whoa!

She closed her eyes, gnashed her teeth, and pictured him with a face full of acne and a horrid case of halitosis.

She let out a giggle and opened her eyes. Damn, he was still dangerously sexy. And tempting.

And she wanted a taste of him.

Quinn took the plate out of her shaking hand and put it on the table. "Ah, Britt," he whispered. Stepping into her, he rubbed his hands up and down her arms, igniting bursts of fire in their wake.

Confusion and need warred within her. "What... what are you doing?"

He was too close... too hot... too damn everything. Britt's heart rate doubled. All thoughts of refusing him vanished. She leaned toward him and placed a hand on his chest to keep from falling.

His presence filled the emptiness she'd been battling for years. It was as if her body knew he'd make all of her previous and often unfulfilling encounters seem tame and uninspired compared to his mere touch. Her thoughts became full of him, and she ached to be closer.

Something wholly elemental took over whenever they were together.

"I'm staking my claim." Quinn's low rumble thrilled her. His head dipped down, his mouth lightly touched her lips, brushing back and forth over her sensitized flesh. He framed her face with his warm hands, pulling her into him and deepened the kiss. He delved deep and fulfilled her wildest fantasy as their tongues dueled and consumed.

Her body in flames, Quinn was the match her long-dormant sexuality had been waiting for. When air became necessary, they broke apart, her chest rising and falling in time to his.

"I've decided Clotho is right, and I'm going to have you," he growled.

His words broke her out of the sensual fog. "Have me?" Still struggling for air, she slapped a hand on his chest. "Listen, this isn't some dating or...or mating game. This is my life. And I'm not your destined anything. Got it? This is just...chemistry."

Quinn spun her around, placed her hands on the countertop. He was rough and gentle all at once.

He pressed his erection against her back, then lower, grinding against the seam of her ass. Britt let out a moan. He was big and hard, and his movements warmed her inside and out. Her craving exploded and need turned into desperation. And then it all clicked. Everything he'd told her was true.

"That sounds an awful lot like a challenge to prove you wrong. I'd be careful if I were you, Britt. Challenge was bred into me. And I fight to win."

Shaking her head, she wanted to shout that it didn't matter anymore. The prophecy, the Fates, even the threat Dante posed. Nothing mattered except being filled by him. She rocked back into his erection, a silent plea to make it happen.

She twisted her neck to look over her shoulder into his eyes, marveling at the emerald green staring back at her. The intense need shining from his gaze triggered a pulsing sensation inside her. Oh my god. Nothing in her past sexual experiences had left her quite so desperate to be taken. The heat between them became too much to bear. She pushed back and twisted herself from his hold until she was facing him. She tore at her blouse, the first two buttons popping off.

"I can't think." She was lost. Frenzied in her need, Britt wrapped a leg around his waist and rocked her hips, seeking relief against his erection.

This was madness.

Her need rose until every reasonable thought she'd given for escaping him was forgotten.

Britt's orgasm built as her hips bucked against him and when she broke, she rode the wave as it faded. He wrapped his hands around her arms and pushed her gently away. Ever so gently that she let out a cry of despair at the separation.

"No... I need you. Now. Inside of me," she begged him.

"Britt, stop. Hell, I almost spilled my seed, lass. We need to stop."

His shout broke the spell. She fell limp and grabbed the counter behind her.

"You need to breathe, lass. Just breathe. That's it, take another."

What the hell was happening to her?

She closed her eyes and did as commanded. His scent was still all around her, and the intense need for him hadn't left, but a new awareness entered her conscience. Something was happening, and he was now inside her head. Soothing words played over and over. What was that?

Somehow, she knew Quinn was giving her the strength to control her emotions. Such an odd sensation to not be in total control of one's thoughts and feelings, yet he didn't take anything away from her, merely added to her abilities. He was able to guide her to bank the burning desire for him while she sensed his mirrored desire was lessening as well. It may be manageable now, but it was still on low simmer.

She opened her eyes to see him pacing on the opposite side of the kitchen. His breathing was labored, more so than hers. His eyes had darkened, and her gaze fell to the front of his pants where his need for her was still very evident. "Let me take care of you." She took a step, and he held up a hand.

"No." Quinn's nostrils flared, and he took in a deep breath. "I was wrong to start this. I thought I'd be able to...but, not here in the kitchen. You deserve better." He ran his hands over his face, the left one tangling in the long tresses her own hands had loosened during her fevered attempt to climb him like a tree.

Her limbs languid from the best orgasm she'd had in years, probably ever, if she were honest, she attempted to focus on what he was saying.

"We also need to get Gavin here to perform the ceremony now that Clotho has given us a timeline. We need to do this right."

She shook her head but couldn't form the words of protest that were on her tongue. Instead, she grabbed a glass next to the sink, desperate for water. Her eyes fell to her shaking hand. She filled it and drank the cool liquid, taking her time to come up with a valid reason to deny him.

Twice she filled the glass. Her thirst sated, she turned back to find Quinn still staring at her, still aroused—still fighting his own need.

Quinn broke first and lifted his face to the ceiling briefly before returning her greedy gaze. She couldn't get enough of him. His jawline, the pulsing, strong, corded muscles in his neck, and his wide stance, which high-lighted his heavily muscled thighs and arms. All of it made her mouth water.

She looked her fill unaware he was doing the same and it took a moment before his throat clearing regis-tered. Her head snapped up to meet his knowing gaze. Her ears were hot, and a flush crept up her neck, inflaming her cheeks.

"There can be no doubt, Britt. We belong together."

SEVENTEEN

Mac strolled into the room, heading for the coffee maker. "What's going on?" He poured off the last of the coffee before looking from Quinn to Britt and back to Quinn. "Um, what did I miss?"

They both ignored Mac's question.

Less than three days remained to get Gavin here and conduct the binding ceremony—all without alerting Dante—before they began the hunt for what was written in the scroll Britt had acquired.

Unmated, she grew more at risk. Dante would stop at nothing to take her away from him and make her his own. The demon would treat her like a broodmare. Creating more monsters like him. Quinn would not let it happen.

The need to take her remained strong and if they were to have sex before the ceremony, their binding would not take. Might never take. Damn the Fates for their messed-up sense of propriety because sex before marriage with your fated mated was a no-no—never mind the hundreds of women they'd all laid with over the millennia they'd been waiting.

No matter how she tempted him, he vowed to keep his hands off of Britt.

"Quinn? Why'd you stop? I—"

"Had to. We must go through the ritual first before we join, that way."

"That way?" Her eyes widened, and she let out a frustrated sigh. "Listen, I'm not sure why my hormones went nuclear, but this need, this ache, it's still there. Less intense but, all I can think about is you. Us. Naked."

Mac cleared his throat. "Uh, still here."

They continued to ignore Mac.

"Ah, lass. I know. And it will increase the longer we are together. Until we are mated. We need to keep a bit of distance between us. But, not for long. I promise."

"Promise. What? This crazy talk of a binding ceremony doesn't work for me. All I want is..." Britt looked toward his brother, noting his grimace. "Sorry, Mac." She paced, rubbing her arms. "It'd be silly to deny ourselves after what just happened. But what I'm not willing to do is tie myself to you forever. I have a life to get back to and—don't look at me like that. I will get my life back."

"Give us a moment." Quinn nodded at an uncomfortable-looking Mac.

Centuries of not believing he would find his mate crashed down on him. He'd endured his existence without someone to share it with and now that he'd found her, he'd do whatever it took to keep her.

It was time to tell her just enough to get her to give him a chance at proving the prophecy true. But what to tell her that wouldn't increase her need to escape?

"Our sire—"

"You call your father sire?" Britt's tone was skeptical.

"Yes. Being a dad wasn't part of the deal."

Sadness mixed with questions appeared in Britt's eyes. Her reaction touched him, but he had to keep his emotions from overruling the destiny entwining them. To go against the Fates now would bring epic consequences. And it might also bring his father back into the fold, and that was something none of the Brethren wanted.

"Wait. Before you tell me something that isn't verifiable, maybe you start with answering my previous question. How many of you are there? Whose Trace, and why is he missing? And maybe also reassure me that where we are now is safe from the demon determined to take me away from you?"

Quinn shifted. He was not used to being questioned. He was the oldest, and thus by default, he was in charge. But he knew she needed the full story. Just then his stomach rumbled reminding him of their interrupted breakfast. "I'll make another pot of coffee, we need food. Sit and eat. What I have to tell you is better handled on a full stomach."

Britt's face was still flushed from her orgasm. He held back a groan, wishing Gavin was already here, wishing he didn't have to battle the Duke of Hell, and wishing he didn't have to tell her about their absent and unpredictable father.

They ate in silence until their plates were empty—the constant buzz of their connection ever-present. Britt sighed after her last bite, her full, soft lips turning up in a smile.

He curled his hands into fists, stood, and walked toward the staircase leading to the basement. "Mac, you need to eat." He waited for a response, but none came. Mac often blocked everything and everyone out while working on a problem.

He took a long breath before returning to the kitchen and his tempting mate. After Mac had his breakfast, they needed to contact Gavin to inform him he'd need to make another trip through the portal sooner than anticipated. Quinn prayed his brother had recovered.

Mac bellowed, "I need both of you down here—now."

"Now?" Quinn shouted back. Shite, his brother had lousy timing.

"It's about the scroll."

"Scroll? Wait, did you go through my bag, Quinn?" Britt's eyes flashed anger.

Quinn found himself on the receiving end of a very pissed-off mate. He remained silent.

Britt sighed in disgust and jumped out of her chair, knocking it backward. "So much for gaining my trust." She ran out of the kitchen toward the staircase.

CHAPTER

EIGHTEEN

Britt descended the stairs. A rush of cool air enveloped her, slowing her steps. The energy change slammed into her, momentarily stealing her breath. She looked around the large cavernous room of exposed limestone bedrock. Her gaze landed on Mac standing next to a table that had seen better days. "Show me," she demanded.

Quinn descended the last step and stood behind her. "Lass, don't blame Mac. He was following my orders."

"Orders! Well, that makes everything better. I wasn't aware this was a military operation, but I guess that weapon you used on the demons should have given me a clue, huh?" Britt whirled to face him and sent the aggravating highlander a look that in her past, had made lesser men think twice in crossing her. She'd used it often when encountering assholes on past digs. And it had no effect on Quinn, because, of course, it didn't.

He wasn't remotely like any man she'd ever come

across. And if he were to be believed, which she was almost a hundred percent there, he wasn't even human. The part of her that should be freaked out about that was half pissed while the other half was...calm, accepting, even a little bit thrilled. It was as if she had stepped into one of her father's made-up adventures.

But she couldn't let him know any of that. Instead, she needed to come up with something more intimidating than a glare to get him to understand she would do anything—anything—even giving in to fate, to maintain control over the information the scroll contained. Hopefully, there'd be time to avoid that route.

However, the nearness of his body and the heat he gave off warmed her against the chill of the room. Her nipples hardened, an ache began between her thighs and dammit, she missed the beginning of Mac's explanation on how he'd broken the cipher.

"I was able to translate most of it and... you're not listening, are you?"

She cleared her throat and stepped away from Quinn. She pulled all of her focus away from him and turned to Mac, striding over to the ancient table where her scroll was spread out. "You aren't the one who needs to apologize, Mac. So, how were you able to translate it so quickly? I've been working on it for months. Actually, going on a year. If I weren't so mad about having it taken from me, I'd be more excited." Britt placed a hand on Mac's shoulder and peered down at the tattered edges of the papyrus. "But I have to admit, I'm impressed, Mac."

In less than a split second, Quinn had followed her

across the room, pulling her tight against his side. His territorial touch and unique scent overwhelmed her senses, and goose bumps erupted along her already sensitized flesh. No, no, no. She was stronger than this, than allowing her desire for him to stamp out her self-preservation. *Get a fucking grip, Dr. Harmony.*

She rolled her eyes at herself but more at Quinn. "This is ridiculous. What are you doing?" she demanded.

Quinn let loose an inhuman growl. Britt looked up in time to catch his pupils change shape and his eyes shift from light to dark green. She watched, fascinated, as he sent a squinty-eyed glare at Mac that had his brother taking several steps back.

"Look, um, yeah. I've got something to check out over there. I'll be right back."

Britt turned her gaze toward Mac as he walked off toward the far corner of the basement. She ignored the highlander as he continued to hold her, and focused back on the scroll. What did Mac find, and what had she missed?

Quinn's sudden jealousy and her stupid hormones aside, she needed to figure out how to get herself, the scroll, and the rest of her things as far away from him as possible. Even as her brain and her heart dueled over which was the right choice, one thing was for sure—she wanted control of her life back.

"Quinn, there's no need to warn your brother off me. Besides, I thought you believed that stupid prophecy crap. That we're fated to mate. So, if it's true, acting like a jealous lover is just idiotic." Britt wiggled out of his reach. She needed to get his mind off of her and the scroll. And she needed time to come up with a plan of escape because right now, she had nothing.

"If you want to make it up to me for stealing my scroll, now would be a good time to spill more of your backstory." Britt's stomach clenched, hoping the distraction worked.

She wasn't sure she wanted to know, but she needed to know what she was up against besides the immortal Brethren, his unpredictable alien sire, and a Duke of Hell determined to take her away from Quinn. Please let that be everything. She wasn't sure she was up for more.

"I mean, don't you think you've stalled long enough? What is it about your father you don't want me to know? I mean, besides that he's from another planet, which makes you half-alien, right?" A new thought struck her as she uttered words that hours ago seemed unbelievable, had she not witnessed his miraculous healing. What was his other half?

His silence ate at her patience. She knew enough about Quinn from the short time they'd been together that if he didn't want to do something, there was no persuading him to change his stubborn mind. Unless she was willing to do something incredibly stupid, like give up her secret in exchange for his truth. Which right now, was not the time. But maybe if she could get him alone and back upstairs. Seduction had never been something she'd been good at. Screw it, she was desperate for information. She gave him her sultriest smile, at least she hoped it was, and ran her gaze over his masculine angles, ripped muscles and a very, stubborn chin.

Shoot.

Britt's question caught him off guard.

It shouldn't have, but lust had set in swift and wouldn't relinquish its tight hold on him until she was truly his. It left him at less than his best, and he struggled for the first time in centuries. The Fates saw themselves as evenhanded, but they were relentless in their demand for him and Britt to fulfill the prophecy they created.

Time was not something they could afford to waste.

She awoke something buried in him, or perhaps brand new. He wasn't used to...to feelings, caring for someone other than his brothers. It made him uncomfortable, and his dragon had begun a constant grumbling to be let out, making it difficult to think.

However, he could no longer deny what was now unquestionable: his need to protect, possess, and cherish Dr. Britt Harmony.

Quinn ran his gaze over Britt's curves. Her eyes

locked on his. Britt's gaze was piercing, imploring him for answers. The look gutted him, realizing how unfair he'd been to withhold information. Her face was still flushed from their earlier encounter, reminding him that neither of them had a say in their destiny, yet he'd slay anyone to ensure she remained his and... shit, he was turning into a sappy human.

The lass challenged him as no other had or ever dared—at least those who hadn't lived long after doing so. He wished he could take her away from here, show her his true self, his dragon half. Away from Dante, and without the interference of the Fates or their father if he ever decided to return.

She deserved the truth.

The truth would protect her.

"Please, Quinn? You say you're immortal, but you surely didn't mean it. I mean, maybe you've been chemically enhanced somehow. Maybe the government's figured out how to—"

"He's gone by many names. Before he disappeared, he went by Tiegh, but you may know him as Thoth, or Hermes, or half a dozen other deities in ancient history. He insinuated himself into various roles of power, and well, it's complicated." Quinn spoke the words in a deep monotone.

"Our father, or sire, as he preferred to be addressed when we were young, arrived here shortly after the Gaelic people began the construction of monuments to the stars and well before the Egyptians gained strength in numbers. Due to the advanced technology of his world, he began to share that knowledge, allowing civilization to advance and thrive at an accelerated rate. He kept the demon race at bay and then successfully confined them to the underworld. No matter his role, the humans worshiped him as a god. At least until he mated with a daughter of Zeus. When we were created, it seems he overstepped what Earth's gods could tolerate, and a power struggle occurred."

The story poured out of him and thankfully she didn't interrupt.

"He quickly found the worship by the humans to be a heavy price and loathed Zeus and his descendants as they often took advantage of humankind. Thankfully it didn't take long for humans to become more self-reliant, thanks to the technology he'd shared with them." Quinn paused as he noted Mac had stopped working in the back of the room, also listening to the story he knew well.

"At great cost to himself, Tiegh used this power of the Universe, and banished Earth's gods to the heavenly plane. And then he too disappeared, and we were left to ensure the demons stayed in the underworld. And we've been doing so ever since."

Britt hadn't uttered a word or tried to interrupt since he began. A look of incredulity graced her beautiful face.

"Who was your mother?" Her words were whispered, rushed, and raspy.

"A goddess. One of Earth's most powerful. She laid with Tiegh six times. We were each born within a fortnight of their mating and fully grown by ten years of age."

"What's her name?" She wasn't giving up.

"Athena."

Quinn noticed Britt's eyebrows raise at his mother's name.

"But she's the Virgin Goddess, Goddess of War, and half a dozen other things. Why would she consent to such a thing? And how were you all kept a secret?"

How was it her father had not told her of her destiny?

He ignored her question. "Before Tiegh disappeared, he assigned each of us a continent to watch over. The castle in Scotland is our base. And there are homes such as this one around the world, making it easier to keep tabs on the humans, and ensure the demon race doesn't rise again. It's been our duty for hundreds of years now. Well, that and searching for our mates."

"So just six of you against all the demons in existence? Wow, those odds suck."

He smiled.

"Actually, we do just fine. Or have until recently. Your discovery of the scroll must have triggered an imbalance of sorts. Dante's powers have increased, as we witnessed yesterday. The time has come for the next generation to be born. Finding our mates before Dante is now our highest priority."

"Wait, next generation? You can't be saying that we, you and me, that I'm going to...No. Just, no. I'm not some broodmare, Quinn."

"It's our duty, lass. And you are not a broodmare. You're one of the keys to not just our survival but humanity's as well. You should see it as a great honor. With your help and the others descended from Brigid, our numbers can increase. And with your help, your gift, locating the tablets will be easier." He cringed at the half-truth. They weren't just missing. They'd been stolen under their watch. They had failed in their sacred duty, waiting centuries to correct. But that part of the story was best left for another time.

"Wait, back up. I'm on information overload here. First, I will not be doing any 'duty' when it comes to having children. I get to decide when I become a mother. And second, tablets? As in more than one? My understanding was there's only one, and that's pure mythology. Just how many are there?" She swiped a piece of hair behind her ear and let out an exasperated sigh.

What was she playing at? His research indicated she knew much more about the tablets than she was letting on.

He decided to let her get away with it, for now. "Initially, there were nine. But it's possible more were made. There are rumors of highly trained and educated humans who learned of their existence and attempted to create duplicates."

"And your father, Tiegh, who was once Thoth, created the tablets?"

Quinn shook his head. "The tablets, three of them, were from his home world and contained vast amounts of knowledge. Secret knowledge his people guarded for millennia upon millennia."

"Earth's secrets, like transmutation? Turning stone into gold, that kind of stuff, right?"

"Nay, more. Secrets of the entire universe."

Her mouth formed a perfect O. "So, um, okay." She began to pace the width of the room. "So, you said there are six of you. I've met Roane, Mac, Gavin, and of course, you. The missing Trace makes five. Who's the sixth?

"Keir. He's currently in Alaska. He prefers to blend in with the humans, and he's on a type of sabbatical."

Mac's snort-laugh echoed off the bare walls.

Quinn's dragon huffed at the sound.

"There were to be twelve of us, but Athena disappeared from our lives after we became full-grown. So, Tiegh made a pact with the Celtic Goddess, Brigid. Her future daughters, or rather, females born of her line, would become mates to the Brethren, thus ensuring the continuance of his line."

At the mention of females, Britt froze and wrapped her arms around her middle. He wanted to comfort her, but he pressed on.

"Unfortunately, Dante discovered the arrangement and got to her first, murdered her when she refused him, then wiped out the remaining Celtic goddesses to ensure no one was left to take her place. Brigid was, is, your ancestor, Britt."

She shook her head. She may deny his words, but deep down, Quinn knew she recognized the truth. "Did your father not tell you about your destiny, lass?"

She shook her head. "He told me bedtime stories, fairy tales, made-up adventures to help me sleep, but..."

An unfamiliar ache enveloped him at her outward distress.

"It was said that Brigid possessed foresight as one of her powers. She knew of Dante's forthcoming attack and sent her son, who she was sure the demon wouldn't think to look for, to hide with a family in the neighboring village. His survival ensured Brigid's line continued. Generation after generation of males carried on until the first daughter was born. You, Britt."

"Wait." Britt held up a hand.

Visibly shaken by his words, she covered her mouth, then tipped her head back, closing her eyes. She was silent so long, he thought she'd gone into a trance.

Her eyes opened, she straightened her back and clasped her hands at her sides. "In one of the stories, a grimoire, or book of spells, was bestowed upon the goddess-witch upon her marriage to a—"

"What, or who was she to marry, Britt?"

"A prince," she choked out.

Quinn prodded, "Just a prince? Where was he from, lass?"

△ △ △

OH, Daddy, why didn't you tell me it was all real? Britt shook her head and whispered, "A Scottish prince, a...a highlander." How could she have forgotten that detail?

The undeniable truth of her father's fairy tales had been staring her in the face since the moment Quinn stepped in front of her.

"She would march through forests and deserts on her quests to return stolen artifacts to the king. And when she was old enough, she would marry the prince, and great powers would then be bestowed upon her."

Quinn lifted Britt's hand. "Or perhaps when the mate is bound to her Brethren mate, her book will appear, and she will become her destiny—a goddess, more than a witch. The mother to the next generation of overseers."

Britt hadn't allowed herself to believe the fairy tales could be real, not really. As a young child, of course, she believed, as most children did, that the world was good, and evil would always be conquered.

But then she witnessed her father's brutal death. If she allowed herself to remember his fanciful stories as an adult, she would push the words away and go on another adventure, another dig looking for relics lost to history.

And then she'd been drawn to Egypt and discovered the scroll now in Mac's possession and a green stone. A shard of emerald. Possibly from a tablet created by beings from another world. And it was still tucked away in her bag, unknown to Quinn.

Or was it?

And where did they go from here?

TWENTY

Dante watched through hooded, bloodshot eyes as the regenerated soul Hades had passed along to him entered his office and placed a bottle of his favorite gin on the desk. A desk made from the bones of the conquered.

The prolific serial killer, Cyrus, had high hopes of being transformed into a full demon instead of the subservient fool he'd become. In the early stages of metamorphosis, he was not quite four feet, with a bulbous head and two stubby horns. His body, or rather its body since it had no genitalia, had long, pale arms and short but muscular legs ending in hooves. The sniveling creature had been dropping off smuggled liquor an attempt to gain Dante's favor. In its bid, its hope, to accelerate the process of becoming a full demon.

It took minor demons centuries to be ready, worthy of the elevation to the soldier class. Cyrus hadn't paid enough in allegiance, but Dante allowed the false hope. It amused and entertained him. He did see something in Cyrus, however. Something that had been missing in his past assistants—a true pleasure in cruelty. Even in hell, that was a rarity. But Cy had no idea what Dante had in store for him.

Even with the future fun at the regenerated soul's expense, the truth was, Dante loathed the lesser demons under his command. They reeked of decay and desperation. A sliver of their humanity remained—fighting for escape.

And then there was the eternal drip of toxic green slime as it wept from the cavern walls, emitting a continuous vapor of old-man halitosis. It overwhelmed the senses. Dante still hadn't gotten used to it in the decades of his exile. Even with his elevated status, luxury he once enjoyed in his time above wasn't afforded him below. Not since he displeased Lucifer.

Officially, he was the seventy-first of seventy-two Dukes of Hell. No chance of becoming anything beyond, but he had aspiration. His beginning may have been at the bottom, but he would do whatever it took to ensure his rise to the top would be soon and permanent. He unscrewed the bottle and poured himself a full glass. He waved his hand and sent Cyrus on its way without acknowledging its efforts or giving it a chance to grovel for praise.

With a wounded look over its shoulder, the minor demon scurried off. Wails of despair bounced off the stone hallway leading down to the level of hell where demons of its class were confined when not in service. The actual hell as described by humans in books and paintings.

Dante's brief appearance on the surface yesterday had increased his irritation with the restraints Lucifer had placed upon him over a century ago—locked and bound to hell. The sentence handed down all because he dallied with the wrong man's wife on the surface in 1914. He'd been undercover in Serbia with a group known as the Black Hand.

His assignment had been to stir dissent and instigate the assassination of Austria's future leader, Archduke Ferdinand. His indiscretion had ignited tempers within the nationalist group intent on takeover, and despite the internal battle his bedhopping had caused, they were still able to kill Ferdinand. The death of the Archduke and his wife had ignited the First World War.

You'd think Lucifer would have been grateful for the new souls the human war had created, but the bastard only cared about being disobeyed. Dante knew his punishment could have been much worse. Yet, his bitterness festered over the decades, as did his hatred for the fallen angel.

Time hadn't been wasted, however, and his plans for the Brethren and Lucifer were now, finally, in motion.

Looking back, he'd served the dark prince with unflinching loyalty in his duties, blindly following in campaign after campaign—for centuries. First, against the gods led by the irritating and arrogant Zeus, then by infiltrating humankind and acquiring soul after soul, sometimes changing the course of fate. And all with little to no reward for his blind obedience.

When he thought he'd done enough that his time had finally come for elevation to Lucifer's inner circle, the Other appeared with technology and abilities far and above any in the underworld possessed. This visitor from the stars would shape-shift his form often—known as Thoth to the Egyptians, Hermes to the Greeks, and finally reinventing himself as a human using the name Tiegh.

But the alien's greatest feat was defiling Athena, the Virgin Goddess. Their mating produced six mongrels whom Tiegh trained before disappearing to subdue the demons and protect the humans.

Dante watched and bided his time.

Then the Fates had spun that damn prophecy.

They decreed the Brethren would be given "mates," fated mates from the descendants of the Celtic Goddess Brigid. These children would join their fathers in the coming war with the underworlds. Another damn prophecy.

Dante had believed he'd solved the problem of Brigid with her death by his hand when she refused to serve him. And then the Fates stepped in—again—and messed up everything. The fucking bitches were next on his list after he handled the Brethren.

A demon assigned in Scotland had encountered a man from the Ancient Artifact Conservatory in a bar. It took several pints, but the idiot spun a tale about a woman, his coworker, who had unerring luck in discovering lost, often mythical ancient artifacts. His bitterness loosened the human's—Greg something—tongue. He was left alive for later use.

The discovery of Dr. Britt Harmony had changed everything. It had been sheer luck that the demon had witnessed the kidnapping firsthand and had noticed the doctor's mismatched eyes. She carried the mark.

Then the attack outside Inverness to take Britt from the Brethren had been a failure. Dante's consolation prize was the joy taken in torturing the sole surviving demon who'd run like a coward after Quinn and the next-in-line brother, Roane, defeated his squad of demon attackers.

Had he been there... no! Rehashing the event made him want to tear something apart. He didn't have time to deconstruct what went wrong or find a lessor demon to torture.

Quinn Smythe is what went wrong. Dante had underestimated the dragon-shifter's capabilities.

It stirred old wounds. It seemed no matter his talents—astral projection, his physical prowess in and out of the bedroom, his clever military tactics—none of it had elevated Dante to where he truly belonged. Where he deserved to be—king of the fucking mountain.

With his first glimpse of Britt, he knew he'd found his destiny. She will bear his child, not Quinn's, and be happy to do so. He earned her dammit, and it was time to take his due.

He would take out every Brethren and eventually their fated mates, save Britt—the Fates be damned.

Scoffing at his melancholy and his ongoing punishment, he rose from the chair, flew over to the ledge, then peered down on his legions, his soldiers who trained endlessly, tirelessly. They'd been given to him to command in hell's battle against the gods and humans. But now, he had different plans.

Leaving hell was the only way to defeat the Brethren, starting with Quinn.

And it meant another deal with the devil himself. And once all his goal's were achieved, he'd end Lucifer as well.

TWENTY-ONE

Quinn's words hung between them. He'd expected her to argue at his declaration, yet Britt's eyes shone greener, brighter with the truth. In his own way, her father had been preparing her for her destiny. Whether she liked it or not mattered little; her acceptance of it was all Quinn needed.

Seconds ticked by as their gazes remained locked until Britt licked her lips. Their plumpness begged for his attention. He closed his eyes for a quick reset. When he opened them after a paltry three seconds of forced sanity, he noticed her shallow breaths matched his, and he wished they were anywhere but in a cold, sterile basement with one of his brothers.

Not touching her stretched him to the point of madness.

She tucked a stray piece of hair behind her ear.

His hands curled.

Then she licked her lips—again.

Damn. Quinn's cock twitched at the movement, and a moan escaped him before he could contain it. It didn't matter the time, the place, or if they were alone. His body wanted, needed her.

"Oh, man. I'd say get a room, but you two need to put some distance between you, like right now." Mac rubbed his face and stood. "I didn't think I'd ever say this to one of my brothers but keep it in your pants, Quinn. At least until Gavin—"

Quinn took a step back from Britt. Mac's words snapped him, if for a moment, out from under the constant state of desire for his mate. He took several deep breaths and strode away from her. The distance afforded him time to focus on her revelation of how close her father's fairy tale was to the prophecy woven by Clotho. But how much more of it had her father told her? Had he told her of the dark days to come?

"Oh my god." Britt's shout had both men looking at her in concern. "I can't believe I didn't think of that." She stepped closer to the table. "Foolish of me," she mumbled.

Mac rushed over to Britt as she pointed at the scroll with a shaking hand.

Quinn's dragon objected with a roar. Thrown off balance by the extreme reaction and his skull pounding from the intrusion, he leaned against the stone wall for a moment. Shite. He understood feelings of protection—it was bred into him. But the intense jealousy both he and his dragon felt made him stronger in a weird, twisted way. She...was...his.

He angled his body away from the stone and strode over to Britt. He placed himself between his mate and brother. The move appeased the still grumbling dragon and righted his equilibrium.

Snickering sounds emitted from his brother. He attempted to ignore them, but as they continued, he leaned around Britt and punched Mac in the shoulder before peering down at the scroll.

"What's wrong?" Looking down at the parchment for the first time, he noticed the faint markings of something so familiar he could draw them in his sleep if need be. The scrolled lines an exact match to each brother's birthmark located between their shoulder blades.

Britt began humming, the tone rising higher. "I've seen this once before. In a much-maligned study on ancient...visitors." She looked between Quinn and Mac.

Neither one said a word or physically reacted.

She let out a sigh. "You know, aliens? I believe it's been associated with Thoth. And wait? Your father. You said he's also known as Thoth, right? This symbol, which is beyond rare, has been found within the great pyramid. You must recognize it?"

Silence filled the cavernous room as each of them stared at the Egyptian symbol of life, an Ankh. The tear-shaped cross was interwoven with an infinity symbol halfway down the stem.

Only descendants of his father and Athena, the Brethren, were gifted with the unique icon.

Mac cleared his throat. "Uh, Quinn. Maybe we better wait until Gavin and the others are here to pursue this further. She needs protection only you can give her."

"What? Don't be silly. Of course, we can carry on. My discovery has nothing to do with the rest of your brothers' arrival. Now that I've seen this, I need to finish deciphering..." She waved her hand over the scroll then finger-combed her hair. "Maybe it'll lead me, well us, to the location, to the—"

"We know the location, Britt," Mac said.

Mac looked at Quinn. "It's no coincidence, is it? We were meant to be here from the very beginning."

Quinn clenched his jaw until he thought his teeth would crack. He'd spent millennia searching for the location of the tablets. Stolen out from under them.

Whenever they had a chance to take their attention from the demons, which had not been often, each of them had searched and followed any clue to the whereabouts of their lost birthright.

"Quinn, do you know what this symbol means? Maybe it's the key to where the emerald tablet is hidden or at the very least where the next clue could be. We need—"

"Aye, we will. But not until the rest are here. Mac inform the others. Have them meet us there at dusk tomorrow."

"But...meet us where? Is this about the ceremony? What aren't you two telling me?"

Quinn's left hand tingled at her upset. He looked down to see it gripped firmly on Britt's hip. He'd barely been aware of it. The need to touch her had become automatic when she was near.

Her warmth seeped into him, fusing them. He absorbed her uncertainty and shivers and pulled her closer. "This is not about the ceremony. Mac seems to think we were meant to be here. That what we are searching for is in the temple."

Her eyes widened at his declaration. A bit of hope shone through.

At that moment, he felt a bit like the god she'd accused him of being earlier. "You're going to get your wish, lass. We need to go back to Chichén Itzá. And we need you to locate its precise location."

CHAPTER
TWENTY-TWO

B e careful what you wish for.

Their location...it was too easy. Britt never trusted easy. Ever.

Everything from the moment Quinn bumped into her... *Kidnapped, Britt. Never forget the hunky highlander kidnapped you.* Since that moment, all her control was lost. Man, she sounded dramatic. *Get over yourself, and take some action.*

Pep talks were never her thing, but she was going to go against everything she'd ever thought to be real, her gift, the years of schooling, her life before her father's death, and leave it all behind in the name of self-preservation.

Because one other thing was also too easy: the missed symbol on the scroll. There's no way she could have missed something like that. And Britt knew it hadn't been there before today.

"Lass?"

Quinn repeated her name louder, "Britt. You okay? I lost you there for a moment."

Britt snorted. *You're going to lose more than my attention, dragon.*

Pasting a smile on her face, she tilted her head. "Just can't believe how fast things change around you two. Are you sure it's safe to go back there? What about the Duke-demon?"

"Dante is probably sulking. He's attached to hell and hasn't been able to physically leave for decades. You have nothing to worry about." Quinn crossed his arms and stood between Britt and the stairs.

For a brief moment, she forgot she wanted to escape. Quinn's shift in stance made the veins pop on his forearms and his biceps bulge as he crossed his arms. What was it about a guy's muscled arms that had her sighing like a schoolgirl? His formfitting Henley outlined every ridge and valley of his torso, and if she didn't get her act together now, she was going to launch herself at him.

"Okay, so no villain to worry over. Great, then I can take a run. I'm feeling all stiff and unsettled from our, uh, um trip. I typically start my days with a run, and I'd like to beat the heat. But I need some tennis shoes."

Quinn immediately shot her down with a grumbly "No," and Mac muttered something that sounded like, "Good luck with that." The younger brother returned to the computer and started punishing the keyboard.

Okay, so no help from him. She prepared herself for

an argument, and if that didn't work, she might have to resort to using something more effective, and doubly dangerous. She'd use their mutual attraction. Using her feminine wiles had never been a problem for her in the past because she was never attracted to any of the men she used it on. Plus, she'd never crossed the finish line— just enough temptation to get obtain information.

But Quinn was a whole different animal tied to a prophecy wrapped up in her life's work. No matter how temptingly life-changing or sexy, the package it was wrapped up in she needed to remember he'd yet to earn her trust and she was keeping her heart heavily guarded.

The real danger lay in her wanting him beyond reasonable control. A simple touch of his arm proved as much. Because if she touched him again, especially after what happened in the kitchen, Britt feared she'd strip on the spot. Which any chance to get rid of the frilly, sleeveless blouse would be welcomed and, oh, duh. That's what she needed to do. And it would get her the precious time she needed to escape.

Seduce Quinn. Because let's face it, her hormones would not stop reminding her they were at red-level status. Besides, she was a grown-ass woman with needs, and she couldn't take it anymore. A few hours of mind-blowing sex was just what she wanted, needed. She'd leave here well-satisfied, energized, and not one bit regretful. And if he were like most males, he'd be out cold after his orgasm, leaving her plenty of time to sneak out, steal the SUV and disappear.

It was the perfect plan. Well, the only plan she could put in play on short notice. And bonus, sex before the dreaded "binding ceremony" would ensure she'd remain free from him and the prophecy. She pushed back the stray thought that he was growing on her, or that she was beginning to actually like him. That kind of thinking would end up getting her bound for life and unable to make her own choices ever again.

She tuned back in to what Quinn was saying, not at all worried he might take her silence for what it was. She stifled a giggle and tried to look interested.

"Dante may not be a worry right now, but that doesn't mean he hasn't sent more of his soldiers. We'll all stay inside until it's time to leave after sundown." Quinn relaxed his arms and turned toward the staircase. "We have a full gym. I'll take you there so you can...work out any kinks. Although, you recovered remarkably quick from your first trip through a portal, I'm surprised you still feel...what was it, unsettled?" He smirked.

I'll give you unsettled. Britt let her gaze land on his taut backside as he climbed the stairs and fanned herself. She followed with a grin and began plotting.

"Must be your genes, lass. Destiny ensured your fast recovery." His tone was confident and slightly smug.

"Hmm. Perhaps." She kept her tone neutral, but on the inside, she was all, *Yeah, you keep thinking that big guy.*

She caught up to him on the landing and dutifully followed him as he showed off a home gym decked out with the latest fitness gadgets. One difference from a professional gym stood out. No mirrors. She guessed men who looked like them had no need or room for vanity. Or maybe they were vampire-highlander-dragon-shifters?

She really didn't know much about any of them to judge what they were fully capable of. Then again, she couldn't let her imagination run too wild. Quinn had saved her from Dante after all.

"So, Trace, the missing brother. He lives here by himself, right? This seems a bit much, don't you think?" She turned in a full circle as she took in the room.

"We all use it when we're here." Quinn gave her a brief side-eye, then powered up the treadmill. "This should give you the workout you're looking for. I'm going back downstairs and help Mac brief the others. I think it best after our time in the kitchen...that we... hmmm...keep our distance. Less temptation."

Oh, no, Mr. Quinn Sexiest-Highlander-Alive Smythe. Distance is the last thing I want right now.

He stood back and gave her a slight bow. "I grabbed a pair of athletic shoes for you. They're up in the closet in our...the bedroom. When you're done, feel free to watch TV or maybe rest. I'll catch you up on our plans over dinner." Quinn didn't pause for a breath as he rattled off directions on using the entertainment system.

"Do you always get your way?" Britt took a step closer to him and leaned on the safety bar, drawing her shoulders back, which lifted her breasts, then stuck her hip out as far as she could without toppling over. She rested a hand on his forearm and waited him out.

She debated licking her lips, but he was smarter than most, and she feared he'd know she was deliberately trying to be sexy. Or maybe... no, he was on to her. She watched his pupils dilate before he lifted an eyebrow and turned his gaze to her hand. It would be all the warning she'd give him today.

She ran her fingers along his arm and stopped just before his elbow. The touch electrified her. Did he feel the same?

She looked up in time as their gazes locked, and he drew in a long, deep breath.

Yeah, he felt the same.

"Playing with fire will only get you burned, mo chridhe." His voice dropped a notch on the foreign word.

Britt had thought she could handle him. The connection. The stupid prophecy. But the whispered endearment had her practically panting for him. It was somehow familiar, but she couldn't place its meaning. "What's *mo chridhe*?"

She drew her hand away and fiddled with her hair, tucking a section behind her ear. Her movement drew his gaze, and she let out a breath she didn't realize she'd been holding. Maybe she didn't need to wait till tonight to seduce him.

Quinn took that option away by taking a couple steps back.

"It's Gaelic and fits you, somehow." He turned and boldly ran his gaze over her bare legs and up, up until their gazes clashed. His eyes were a dark green, like they'd been earlier when he had his hands all over her.

The one consolation from his refusal to take the bait was she now realized how much the strain of keeping his hands off her was, and that he was as wrapped up in this crazy hormonal need as her—perhaps more.

Hopefully more.

"Sooo... Chichén Itzá, huh?" Britt cleared her throat and tried to ignore her pounding heart. "Don't you think the coincidence is too much?" Her brain finally kicked in, thank god, and she went with it. "That the place you bring us to is the very place where the answers you've been searching for centuries... I mean, it's just too easy."

His silence was maddening. She went a step further. "Dammit, Quinn. I thought we were fated mates. Couples, partners share things. What if—"

"The sooner you stop questioning the Fates, and perhaps use a bit of patience, the sooner your answers will—"

"That's a bunch of crap and empty words, Quinn. I'd hoped you would be honest with me. Holding knowledge hostage is so not the way to begin a relationship in case you weren't aware." Her frustration chased away the lingering effects of their earlier touch, and she used it to push him.

"What if the tablet isn't there? Huh, what then? And what if the Fates are wrong?"

He paused. It was barely noticeable, but she seemed to break through his tough guy act. Then he left the room with her questions ringing in her ears. Damn.

Britt wanted to shout "coward" at his retreating back but held off. She didn't want to go too far in antagonizing him.

Although wholly instigated by her, their little fight was the perfect way to approach him later with a tried-and-true solution—make-up sex.

TWENTY-THREE

Unsettled with no immediate physical outlet or a demon to rip apart, sitting down for dinner held no appeal as Quinn watched Mac place a platter of ribs in the center of the table.

The cause of the unfamiliar emotion sat to his right. Britt's reaction to him earlier in the day played on repeat, nonstop.

His cock was in a near-constant state of readiness whenever she was close, and to his chagrin, a mere thought of her had him at half-mast as he replayed the day in between strategizing with Mac and his brothers.

Quinn shifted as Britt's arm brushed his.

"Sorry." Her mumbled apology rang hollow.

He suspected she was up to something even as her questions from the morning still rang in his ears. Quinn desperately wanted to show her a better way to use her mouth than questioning his every move. If she could just use some patience, all the information she wanted would be transferred telepathically to her once they mated. Just as all of his father's knowledge had passed to his mother when they first mated.

So, if she wanted to play, he'd be ready. No matter how difficult she made it for him, he would hold her at arm's length until they were officially mated—until he was able to bury himself balls deep inside her curvy body.

Quinn's dragon woke as images of Britt beneath him played out in his mind. *Shall we show her now?*

Nay! He pushed his beast back under. There were rules. One of them needed to follow through on the decree by the Fates. He'd keep his hands off her until Gavin performed their binding ceremony, even if he had to keep Mac with him 24/7 as their chaperone. Thankfully, he only had another day to wait.

He offered Britt the plate of ribs, and their fingers grazed. His gaze snapped to her face, and the blatant need in her eyes nearly did him in.

Quinn couldn't imagine waiting a moment longer to make her his. Shite, this was going to be the longest fucking night of his very long life.

⚠ ⚠ ⚠

BRITT DIDN'T KNOW what to say or how to act during dinner. Mac was sitting across from her, which made things awkward. Her seduction plans did not include having a chaperone listening to every word she spoke.

Not that she said much. And she managed to eat even less. Her stomach tight, she listened as the two brothers discussed their strategy for tomorrow. The rest of their brethren would use the portal and arrive shortly before dawn, meeting them at the temple.

Frustrated, she excused herself and took their plates to the sink. She washed a few dishes and continued to listen as they plotted.

Enough was enough. "It's getting late. I'm...uh...I think I'll turn in. 'Night." Britt dried her hands and stepped toward the hallway, then paused. Letting her head fall back, she scolded herself for wimping out. Straightening her shoulders, she turned and cleared her throat.

"Quinn? Um, I'd like to speak with you when you two are done. Alone. In, uh, our bedroom." She sent him a slow and hopefully seductive smile. Tucking a piece of hair behind an ear, she let her hand trail down the side of her body before giving him a wink. Sure, it was obvious, but she no longer had the luxury of time. Not that she ever had.

Mac laughed, then covered his mouth with his hand. Quinn glared at him.

Quinn turned to her and their gazes locked. She held her tongue, waiting until he responded. His features remained guarded. But that was nothing new. Britt let her gaze land on his lips before moving over his upper body and stopping on his hands. A flash memory of how those hands brought her pleasure earlier in the day made her grin.

"Shit, Quinn. You're in trouble." Mac's mumbled words rang out in the still room.

Yes, he was, she silently agreed.

Quinn gave her a brief nod, and she took it and walked away before he asked her what was so important. She kept her fingers crossed as she entered the bedroom, eyeing the big bed and debated whether to lie down and wait for him or not? A bit obvi, so she decided against it and went into the adjoining bathroom to freshen up.

She went into the closet and repacked her bag, making sure the case with the emerald was still there. She'd squirreled away supplies earlier in the day while Quinn and Mac had remained downstairs. Confident she had enough to get her to a large enough city with an airport and freedom, she finished getting ready.

Splashing cool water on her face and brushing out her hair, the sound of Quinn entering the bedroom reached her. "You've got this, Harmony," Britt whispered to herself before opening the connecting door and stepping into the darkened room. She'd left only one table lamp on. Its soft glow bolstered her courage.

"Hi," she said. Not her best opening line.

"I know what you're up to, lass." Quinn leaned against the door frame and crossed his arms. "Don't get me wrong, I'm eager to bed you as well, but we will follow tradition and wait." His gaze landed on the bed. "You already know I want you. You and no other, Britt. However—"

"Anyone ever tell you that you talk too much?" She

took a shaky step forward and unfastened the top button of her blouse.

"You don't want to do this." Quinn pushed off the wall, setting his stance. His hands curled, and his nostrils flared.

"Oh, but you want me too, don't you? This strange connection we have tells me so. You want me to be the one to say 'screw the consequences' and deal with whatever comes—later. Because breaking that damn prophecy won't keep us from taking what we want—each other naked in that bed—on our terms."

Emboldened, she took the remaining steps to come within his reach. She absorbed his body heat and accepted that the unique waves of energy and the sexual craving she felt whenever they were this close, were meant only for her.

She may accept that fate meant them to be together, but she'd be damned if the Fates ruled her. Them.

Reaching out before she could talk herself out of it, she ran her hands over his crossed arms and up the contours of his biceps. She snaked one hand over his shoulder up to his neck while her heartbeat kicked into high gear from the skin-on-skin contact. She licked her lips and wound a hand into his long, silver locks and behind his head. Tipping her face up, she hesitated a moment as fear overtook her that he'd push her away.

His gaze locked on her lips, he ground out her name on a low growl. The sound enveloped her and wrapped around her heart. She refused to call it love, but it tripped an emotion she'd never felt—as close to bliss as she'd ever been.

Britt cupped his face, guided him down to her eager mouth, and pressed her lips against his.

Hot.

Demanding.

She sipped, she nipped and sucked his lower lip, then slipped her tongue between his lips.

Into the kiss, she poured years of loneliness, memories of yearning to be the young girl fashioned into a fairy tale, then finding acceptance and love from a highland prince she'd dared believe could be real.

And he was real.

A darker, larger-than-life, more mysterious version.

Destined or not, he was hers.

Quinn took over the kiss and devoured her. Breathing seemed irrelevant. Their tongues dueled, igniting a burst of electricity, increasing the ache for his touch on her breasts and between her thighs.

A moan shuddered through her. Desperate to touch him, she tunneled both hands under his shirt, wrapping her arms around his waist, stroking his muscled back, and held on. No longer in control of her planned seduction when he tipped her head back to deepen their kiss, she happily gave him all that he wanted.

Suddenly, Quinn yanked on her blouse, the remaining buttons popped off and fell to the floor.

"I'll buy you a new one." His voice was thick with desire.

She gasped at the shock of the cool air on her flesh

before he covered her breasts with his roughened yet warm hands. The contrast stoked her need for more. When he answered her silent plea and flicked his thumbs over her already hard nipples, she rejoiced.

He rested his forehead on hers and took in deep lungfuls of air.

"You are mine, and I am yours. Never forget that."

She arched into him and squirmed. His words— unnecessary. Britt needed him to move his hands farther down, to touch, and to burn his heat into her. Every pulse point on her body fired off. Her breath caught in her throat, butterflies erupted within her and a warmth pooled in her lower abdomen. Desperate for the release only he could give her.

"Quinn." Her whispered plea was surprising and desperate to her ears. "I need—"

"I know, lass. I feel it as well. What is between us is more than I could have ever predicted. It's too much and not enough all at the same time, but we have to wait and—"

"Nooo." Her response shocked them both. Sure, her plan was to seduce and have the experience of her life before she left him in the dust, but this...it was beyond everything she dreamed. Their connection felt... unbreakable.

And as hot as their time in the kitchen had been, it was nothing compared to this moment. This moment was—molten. She knew it would only get better. She couldn't stop now if she wanted to. God, he better not stop either.

Looking up at his face, she noticed the corner of his mouth lifted at her moan as he continued to rub slow circles over her aching nipples. Yes, her body screamed. Britt rolled her hips, searching for more contact, and he chuckled.

She absorbed his deep rumble and grasped his forearms to hold herself steady. "No waiting. I need you, Quinn. We're in charge of our lives, damn the Fates."

"You're playing with fire, lass. When Clotho and her sisters are denied, you dinna want to be in their path."

Quinn's words infuriated her. She no longer cared if she got away from him—all she wanted was him. The future would take care of itself.

She literally felt drunk on Quinn. Now that he had his hands on her again, she wasn't going to let him talk himself, or her, from the pleasure of feasting on the other. If she couldn't convince him with her touch, she'd use her words.

"Quinn, I can't stop thinking about earlier. You got me off, and it only seems right that I do the same for you." She ran a hand down the front of his pants and stroked his erection.

Britt sensed his inner battle, and she was going to use that against him. Surely, whoever decreed that they go through a stupid ceremony before they had sex never experienced this level of need. And her need to have his cock inside her, pounding into her...was...it was as if she could already feel him within her. Her inner walls spasmed in anticipation.

Groaning in response, he bent down, taking turns

rolling his tongue over her nipples, kneading the undersides of her heated flesh.

"Quinn. Please. I need more. I need you."

The room tilted as he picked her up and carried her to the bed. She heard him mumble incoherently. He placed her gently in the middle of the mattress, stood back, and looked at her.

She peered at him through hooded eyes and sucked in a short burst of air at the greedy need in his gaze as it roamed over her. She reached out to him. He shook his head as if lost in a debate she didn't want him to win.

Exhaling as he kneeled over her, she grinned when he braced his elbows on either side of her. She had no time to gloat over winning this battle as he bent down and feathered his lips between her breasts, down her ribs, her stomach, then twirled his tongue inside her navel, wringing a cry of pleasure from her.

She was on fire. But she didn't need the foreplay. She laid her hands on his shoulders. "Please, Quinn, please touch me."

With a groan, he answered, "So demanding." Dropping a kiss onto her mound, he lowered her panties.

She wiggled her hips as he guided the scrap of material down her legs before tossing them over a shoulder. Before she had time to think, he delved his tongue inside her and suckled her swollen flesh.

Britt screamed his name and reached down and parted herself. His tongue flicked back and forth. His strokes wrung tiny, sharp cries from her. She rocked her hips against Quinn's wicked tongue and closed her eyes.

She was on the verge of orgasm as he sucked her tight bud back into his mouth, then the first wave hit. Britt bucked wildly.

He increased the pressure, and a shudder racked her body. Quinn squeezed her hips, holding her tight as he kept up a campaign of pleasure. Her inner walls grabbed his tongue, and as he inserted a finger and stroked her, she grasped the sheets in her fists and called out his name again as she broke and then crested, riding wave after wave of a divine, tingling current.

The orgasm overtook her, and yet he didn't stop. Not until she came a second time as he worked her clit until stars erupted behind her eyelids.

It still wasn't enough.

She wanted, needed him inside her.

Dazed, Britt watched as Quinn peppered her stomach with open-mouth kisses and sweet words. Noticing he still had his clothes on, she reached down, snaking her hands between them. Fumbled with his belt, found his zipper, and freed his erection.

He leaned to his side, giving her full access to his cock. Thick and long, she grasped him gently. Keeping her gaze on his, she twisted her hand around its velvety length.

"Lass...Britt." He released a hiss and bucked into her hand. "Sweet temptress, stop, or I'm going to spill my seed like a damn teenager."

Instead, she increased her pressure and began stroking him from his balls to the tip of his rock-hard shaft. She wasn't giving him any time to deny her. Britt watched, fascinated as his whole body shuddered from her touch. Quinn's reaction excited her, and as his moans mingled with hers, she increased her speed.

Quinn circled her wrist and squeezed. "Britt, release me," he said, his tone ominous.

No, this wasn't how it was supposed to go. "Quinn, please, we can't stop now."

The highlander didn't respond. Instead, he held her gaze, fire burning in his eyes as she was overcome with a compulsion to release him.

"Your clever touch nearly had me coming. And if I'm to do so, it will be buried so deep inside you, *mo chridhe*, we'll not know where the other begins."

Britt's heart near burst, and her body lit up at his words.

Quinn kicked off his boots, removed his pants, and pulled his shirt off so quickly, her mind could barely follow his movements. Her eyes widened as she ate up every inch of his sculpted body. He didn't give her long to admire him as he covered her once more, placing a knee between her legs nudging them open. She was quivering with anticipation. Quivering. Her.

He leaned down to suck on one of her nipples. She groaned and lifted herself higher. He nipped and licked the tip before giving its twin the same attention. Britt's eyes crossed. Closer, she needed him closer. She wrapped her legs around his waist and rocked her core into his erection. He stilled and lifted his head.

The look he gave her triggered a rush of liquid between her thighs. "Now. I need you inside me, Quinn."

She watched in amazement as the color of his emerald eyes darkened further.

Without a word, he captured her lips and ran a hand between them, taking his cock in his hand and lining it up to her entrance, rubbing the tip back and forth between her sensitive folds.

With his tongue, he mimicked the movement of his cock between her legs. The short strokes, in and out, drove her crazy, yet she didn't want the sensation to end. When it did, she wanted to cry, but he guided himself inside of her, and slowly, ever so slowly, he filled her.

When he pulled out and filled her again, Britt let out a sigh. She matched the rhythm he set, running her hands along his thighs and over his ass, pulling herself closer.

Quinn increased the speed of his strokes and rubbed his thumb over her clit, sending her into a freefall as spasms erupted, triggering an intense orgasm. She shouted his name and squeezed his cock, rocking her hips in a frenzy.

Quinn roared as he reached his peak and, as promised, spilled his seed within her. Their bodies rocked and settled in unison. Lulled into a contentment that quickly became a craving to do it again, Britt was instantly slammed with an overwhelming sense of knowing. It was immediately followed by a flood, a download of information. From Quinn.

Time stopped.

Memories were imprinted into her brain.

Quinn's memories.

Years of learning, searching, and living were all revealed to her.

And the truth of the prophecy, his lineage, and her place in the battle against the demons rang clear and true within her.

With Quinn still inside her, had the process of binding just happened without the much-discussed ceremony? Because she was certain that what they just shared and the info dump swirling within her was supposed to happen after his brother performed the official binding.

The binding she'd meant to avoid by having sex with Quinn before the ceremony.

Shock filled her as she realized she was now truly bound to this man who wasn't merely a man but part god, part other with a dragon side she wasn't sure she was ready to deal with.

And if she knew everything he knew, had ever known, did that also mean he knew her memories and, more importantly, her secrets?

TWENTY-FOUR

Quinn's dragon roared. Images, feelings, and a plan for escape slammed into his skull. He'd done the unthinkable. He'd buried himself in Britt and planted his seed. His body convulsed at the connection, the effing satisfaction and unmatched experience of their mating outweighed whatever price he would pay for defying the Fates of their precious binding ceremony.

He hovered over his mate, making sure to keep his weight off her as he let the moment wash over him. He took in her startled gaze as the transfer of information continued to flow between them.

Would it never end?

All he wanted was to begin loving her again and witness her pleasure as she accepted him inside of her, giving him another chance to ensure she became pregnant. But the damn beast within wanted free.

His dragon also had a need—to show his mate his

other half and gain her acceptance. Quinn battled the uncertainty of their coupling without the ceremony produced. He wouldn't be surprised if all three of the Fates appeared at the foot of their bed poised to punish them.

As if a switch had been flipped, the images between them stopped. He threw his head back, and he let out a roar that rattled the windows. He settled on his back next to Britt, drained physically and mentally.

He felt Britt's body shudder. He turned and watched her through new eyes as her chest rose and fell, no doubt processing their mating, as was he. Before he could form words to tell her what she meant to him, she sat up in bed, her hair mussed and flowing over her shoulders.

She was glorious.

Quinn captured her wild gaze. Her eyes glowed, like his, but she seemed oblivious to the change.

"That shouldn't have happened. How could it?" Britt scrambled out of bed without a backward glance, scooped up her clothes, and ran into the bathroom. The slamming of the door rattled the wall. Followed by a tortured wail and cursing.

So much cursing.

He jumped from the bed. "Britt!" He tried the doorknob. Locked. He pounded on the solid wood. "Open this door, lass."

Silence.

What the hell? This was not how he expected his mate to respond after what had just occurred between them. No pillow talk. No basking in the afterglow. No demands for an explanation for all the information she just received.

And why did the transfer still happen? They hadn't gone through the binding ceremony. Something didn't feel right.

"Clotho! Show yourself!" His bellow rattled the doorframe.

The Fate did not appear.

He hadn't expected her to.

But he still wanted answers.

And so did his dragon.

There was no holding it back at this point. He could feel the change pulling at his skin. The tightness turned to pain and unless he allowed it to happen, he'd shift inside the house and the chance he would injure Britt during the process were unacceptable.

He pounded another fist on the door. "You want to see my dragon, lass?" His voice cracked, its tone deep and guttural. Speech was always the first to go.

Still silent. Dammit.

No time to wait for her response, Quinn bolted from the room, running for hidden door off the kitchen. It was still dark outside, dawn a couple of hours away. He could just make it.

Trace had purposely built the house far enough from the humans, so when they shifted, the chances of discovery should be zero.

The night air skimmed his heated flesh as he ran. Scales appeared and his bones popped. He continued to run till his legs made the final change, and he leapt into the sky. His wings gaining lift, Quinn, now fully dragon, soared through the empty sky, reaching the coastline in mere minutes.

He followed the peninsula at top speed. Shifting into dragon form had become increasingly dangerous over the decades due to the humans' technological advances. Each brother had been forced to keep their other halves under tight rein. They only changed into their alternate form during battle and when at least one other of their brethren was present to assist in creating a cloaking field large enough to avoid detection.

Quinn was taking a great chance as he flew over the Yucatan, but neither he nor his dragon gave a fuck at the moment.

It had been years since he'd flown. The joy pumping through his dragon's veins matched only by the moment Britt had become his mate when he'd planted his seed within her.

Guilt could come later. For now, he and his dragon soaked in the freedom and the triumph of finally taking a mate.

He needed to return and reassure her and introduce her to his dragon.

Quinn banked toward the compound and opened his thoughts to hers. Not sure how much time had passed since their joining, he was picking up mumbled words. He sent her what he hoped were soothing words; this all so new to him. He waited for a response.

And waited.

Finally, about five miles out from the house, her

voice rang loud in his mind, and if a dragon could grin, then the tightness he felt around his elongated snout must be an indication that yes, a dragon could grin. From her choice of words, his mate was having a major fit over his absence.

Quinn pushed another thought toward Britt. "Lass. Meet me behind the house. And make sure you're dressed. I'm sure even Mac couldn't have slept through all the noise and I don't want my brother seeing you unclothed."

Her response was instant, and her words no longer sounded as if they were produced underwater. This time they were crystal clear.

"Damn you, highlander. Where are you?"

He grinned again.

Patience was never going to be one of his mate's strong suits.

Quinn circled the house and spotted Britt on the small back patio. She wore one of his t-shirts, the fabric hitting her mid-thigh. Her loose hair whipped around her head from the wind created by his wings. Her expression was blank, yet through their connection, he felt her worry and anger at him leaving.

Ready to land, he sent Britt a warning through their telepathic link. "Look up, and prepare."

His almond-shaped glowing green eyes zeroed in on her as she shook her head before lifting her chin to the sky.

The ground shook as Quinn landed, sending up a small plume of dust along the desert floor surrounding the compound. He scanned the area for trespassers and thankfully found none.

He picked up Mac's heat signature as his brother stepped from the shadows. Quinn settled his wings tight against his giant form. His talons clicked together as he settled. "You wanted to see my dragon, lass. Well, our mating has now granted you that opportunity."

He readied himself for an argument as their gazes met.

Unprepared for what happened next, he shouted for Mac as his mate's eyes rolled into the back of her head. Britt wobbled, then dropped, her head bounced once and settled onto the hard-packed earth.

Quinn lost at least a century from his life watching her fall. He lowered and angled his head to nudge her too-still form. Fear that she'd injured herself overcame him.

He begged the Fates for forgiveness and pleaded with her to wake. "*Mo chridhe*...please open your eyes. Yes, that's it, sweetheart. Just breathe for me."

Britt stirred. The slight movement relieved him as she let out a low groan followed by a sneeze. Her body, so small and frail next to his in dragon form, stirred his protective instincts. All he wanted to do was scoop her up and take her back to bed and reassure her, then once again bury himself deep within her. But they needed to get this first meeting over with.

Her acceptance of his dragon half meant more to him than his very existence. Without it meant a battle he was unsure he could win.

CHAPTER

TWENTY-FIVE

Britt's head rang with Quinn's voice. Blinking slowly, she rolled to her side and faced the creature she saw while in the portal. Glowing green eyes bored into her. Iridescent scales shimmered from the glow of the waxing moon.

Quinn was nowhere to be seen.

Larger than the structure behind her, the dragon's head was too close for comfort. His head was bigger than her first car. Blinking her eyes to clear the dust stirred up by the dragon's landing, she attempted to focus on the beast's features.

Ridged brows and flared nostrils, its almond-shaped eyes glowed green. Mesmerized, she watched silently as his gaze roamed over her. The color of the magnificent creature's eyes matched only one person, and for that reason, she didn't freak the hell out.

Instead, she reveled in the harsh beauty of the dragon and the fact it wasn't trying to eat her. Britt

177

pushed herself up into a sitting position and looked around the yard, bathed in moonlight. She lifted her hand to brush the dust from her hair and arms. Where was Quinn?

"Easy, lass. That was quite the bash your head just took."

She whipped her head around, searching. "Quinn?" Where was he? And why did his voice sound far away?

"In the flesh. Well, under a layer of armor." Quinn chuckled.

Mac stepped out of the shadows. "Sorry to interrupt, but I expected more of a reaction, brother. Since she's calm, I'll go back to my warm bed. We still have a couple hours before our brethren arrive."

Britt jumped at Mac's words. "Wait, where's Quinn? Mac, get your butt back here. Aren't you the least concerned there's a dragon in your backyard?"

He paused and looked first at her, then the dragon. "Nay. You seem to be fine. Besides, you two have a lot to discuss."

Britt shook her head and stood, brushing more dirt from her arms and Quinn's shirt. "Mac, where's Quinn, dammit?"

He kept walking.

She braced her fists on her hips. "Highlander! Show yourself!"

"I'm gonna bet that you're not the one in danger, Britt." Mac let out a low chuckle, then disappeared through the hidden door she'd just exited.

"Lass, I'm right here."

Again, she heard Quinn's voice, but not with her ears. The words filtered through her mind as if she was conversing with him in a dream. But this was no dream. Fully awake, her head pounded, and she choked on a mouthful of dirt as she opened her mouth to yell once more.

"Britt, I need you to calm yourself."

Sputtering, she whirled on the creature behind her. "Calm? I am calm. This is me being calm." She folded her arms and faced a creature that till this moment she'd only seen or read about in fiction books.

"So, the vision I had in the portal was real, right?" It wasn't meant to be a question because the dragon was undeniably real, although she desperately wanted someone to jump out and yell "April Fools."

No answer.

Maybe this was all a bad dream.

Could a dragon smile? Maybe it was more of a grin. The beast didn't say anything, but he...or it, was definitely smiling. Frustrated and uncertain what to do next, she closed her eyes and began counting backward from twenty. She got to five when the voice in her head interrupted her.

"Four, three, two, one. Open your eyes, sweetheart. I'm still here. And I'm real as you are."

No, no, no. She didn't want any of this to be real. All she wanted to do was get herself and the scroll and her piece of emerald and go back to her safe, mostly uneventful life in London and forget that she ever traveled to Scotland, was kidnapped by a hot highlander, escaped a demon ambush, met a Duke of Hell, then had amazing sex with the same highlander who claimed she was his mate.

And most of all, she wanted to forget all the information dumped into her conscious.

She picked up a loud chuffing noise and the clicking sound that could only be coming from the direction of the non-imaginary dragon. Britt opened her eyes and let out a long sigh. "Quinn?"

Midnight and emerald green scales rippled along the neck of the dragon as it nodded its head.

"Aye, tis me."

Britt clenched and unclenched her fists. Okay, so her lover was a dragon-shifter. No big deal, right? Actually, there'd been enough clues dropped to warn her. His magical sword, the castle, the symbols, and the childhood fairy tales her father had weaved.

"Come closer, lass."

She wasn't sure she wanted to. Even after all that had occurred, what if the creature wanted to eat her instead of just talking to her?

"Only in human form, Britt."

The thought in her head was followed by a rumbly chuckle that reminded her that Quinn had done just that not too long ago. She squeezed her thighs together at the memory.

"But I need you to get to know my other half. My dragon half."

She jumped at the foreign intrusion of her thoughts. "Okay, so I'll accept the telepathy, but if you tell me you're going to be reading my thoughts whenever you want, that's a deal-breaker."

"I can only read your thoughts when I'm in this form. It's for your safety in case we're unexpectedly separated. Think of it as a built-in safety feature."

A built-in safety feature, um yeah, that's a big no. But at the moment, what choice did she have?

"Okay, so let's say I'm down with you being half-dragon. What's next? Where do we go from here?" Britt couldn't believe she was holding a conversation with a dragon. Waiting for his answer, she moved her gaze over the beast's back with its single row of spikes. She marveled at the club-shaped tail covered in spear-shaped bones. From the corner of her eye, she picked up on movement.

Fascinated, she watched as the dragon stood and stretched to its full height, unfolding black, leathery wings. Any sane person would be running in the opposite direction at the display of power and strength, but all she saw was grace and beauty.

Britt absorbed the undeniable connection as it washed over her, confirming the magnificent beast was indeed Quinn. Her mate.

"Care for a ride, lass?"

TWENTY-SIX

A ride? A chill tripped down Britt's spine. Did she dare confess her fear of heights?

Rarely at a loss for words, she opened then closed her mouth. Flying around on the back of a dragon. Could she?

She'd been born an adventurer. Wanderlust flowed in her veins. Her father had instilled the wonder of what the world had to offer. Then, after his murder, the need to travel and discover new and old things had kept her going—kept her from falling into despair as she pursued her archeology degree. The pull of finding lost treasure was bred into her. She thrived on adventure.

And deep in her bones, she'd felt the magic from a very young age. A magic she kept tamped down and hidden from everyone.

Her father explained it was her heritage—her Celtic destiny. A concrete connection to her father's fairy tales.

But a ride on the back of a dragon? Um, yeah, that had to be a big fat juicy no.

"Lass? We've not much time before sunrise." The dragon stepped closer and lowered its magnificent head.

"I, uh. Can I get back to you?" Britt clasped her hands in front of her. "I need a minute, maybe a month to ah... digest this." She waved her hands in giant circles toward the man who wasn't a man, but a dragon the size of a motorhome. Make that two motorhomes.

A breeze fanned her face while waiting for him to speak telepathically or whatever. It could have only come from one place. One creature.

Quinn...or damn it, the dragon let out several chuffing noises as his response. Was the dragon pouting because she wasn't jumping up and down at his offer?

Too bad because there was no way in hell she was climbing on the beast for some type of joy ride, even if it was Quinn.

A loud rumble rang out. Britt absorbed the vibration as the dragon's laughter ran through her body.

"Perhaps another time then. You've handled all that's been thrown your way till now fairly well."

Britt released a long sigh. "Thank you. So, are you going to—"

Between one moment and the next, the moonlight shimmered and rolled in waves over her dragon—*wait, her dragon?*—then Quinn's naked form appeared. She blinked several times, then took in the hard planes and valleys of the highlander as he rose from a crouch and marched toward her.

Her mouth dropped into an O. Her gaze locked onto the area below his chiseled abs.

"I hope you've recovered from the shock of meeting my dragon, lass. After I shift, you'll find that my need for you will be greater than normal. And lucky us, we have a bit of time before meeting up with my brothers."

This was not how she thought her night would go. The hope of her planned escape had vanished when she woke after Quinn had—yes, it's a cliché, but damn, that immortal rocked her world. Seeing him now, ready for another round, almost erased the memory of what she'd just witnessed.

Almost.

"Um, not that I don't want to tango again, but don't you think we should at least talk about—"

Britt let out a squeal as Quinn scooped her up, anchoring his hands under her ass, pulled her into his hard body, and kept walking. He captured her lips in a deep, desperate kiss, knocking her senseless.

The hidden door opened as they approached. She didn't have time to process how he'd managed that trick.

Stomping down the hall to their bedroom, Britt felt a tug at the back of her skull.

Quinn's thoughts popped into her brain—naughty and inventive. Apparently he'd fibbed about the telepathy thing only happening when he was in his dragon form. She'd let it go...for now.

Their lips still fused, she wrapped her arms around

his neck and held on for dear life. She couldn't get close enough to him.

Just a few more steps.

"Quinn." Mac's voice held regret and a tinge of something she couldn't get a handle on.

Her highlander kept walking, ignoring his brother's plea. Quinn kicked the door shut in Mac's face, then stopped at the end bed and let go of her. Still clinging to his neck, Britt let her legs fall from his hips, relaxed her arms, and shimmied her body slowly down his front, bumping into his erection. An appreciative groan of pleasure rumbled from him.

Britt wiggled her hips, rubbed herself against him again, earning herself a firm slap on her right butt cheek. The unexpected but welcome stimulation sent a wave of warmth through her with an added bonus spasm in her girly region. She broke the kiss and locked eyes with him. "Yes, please."

Quinn's emerald-green eyes glowed, piercing her with a molten look. Then, with a gentle push on her shoulder, she fell back onto the rumpled sheets.

She lifted herself onto her elbows and waited. Talking was overrated anyway. They'd figure things out. Later.

She held Quinn's gaze while he reached down, grabbed the hem of the oversized t-shirt she wore, whipping it off her body. He climbed up the bed, ran a hand up the inside of her thighs. Her legs fell open as she watched him lower his head.

"Sorry to interrupt, but your brother did try to warn you."

"What the fuck!" Quinn roared. Jumping from the bed, he crossed the room for his sword. Swinging it over his head, his gaze roamed the large room, seeking out the intruder.

Britt grabbed the comforter and covered herself, scrambling up onto her knees. She pushed a chunk of hair out of her eyes, "Quinn, no!" Chest heaving, Britt stared in embarrassment at the woman standing calmly in a corner of the room.

Britt looked back toward Quinn. His eyes glowed from beneath the long hair hanging in front of his face. The tieback he used was long gone after his shift in and out of dragon form.

"Mother! Shite, what are you doing here?" Quinn growled, tossing his weapon on the bed. He found a pair of jeans and tugged them on, not bothering with a shirt.

Mother? Britt took another look at the woman in flowing robes, standing regally in the corner of Quinn's room. She towered over her son by a good foot.

Her long raven hair arranged in an elaborate updo was woven around a golden crested helmet.

Her features were striking.

Her presence was intimidating, and she was staring at Britt with a knowing smile.

Athena, the Greek Goddess of Wisdom, Warfare, Handcraft, and a half-dozen other titles, had seen her naked?

Had seen her having sex with Quinn. Okay, almost having sex with the goddess' son.

Could this night get any stranger?

TWENTY-SEVEN

"*Tsk-tsk*. Language my son."

"What? How?" Britt's voice cracked, echoing off the stone walls.

Quinn ignored his mother and looked over to Britt. Up to this point, she'd handled his transformation better than anticipated, but an eight-foot goddess? Even he was taken aback at her timing.

"I'd like to know that as well." He crossed his arms and waited.

Athena didn't appear in a hurry to enlighten them. Her features relaxed as she ran her fingertips over the fluffball perched on her left hand. Quinn searched his memories for the owl's name. When he came up blank, he threw out his arms. "It's been over a century. What brings you out of exile?"

Patience was not one of his strong points, plus he was worried about Britt. She clutched the comforter tightly against her chest. He zeroed in on her rapid breaths and the squinting of her eyes. He looked around the room for her glasses. Locating them, he snagged them off the dresser and handed them to her.

"Lass." Quinn smiled as she perched them on her nose.

Wide-eyed, Britt cleared her throat. "Exile? But you're a god...goddess, who is powerful enough?"

Quinn needed to cut this conversation short. He wasn't interested in hearing about his mother's ongoing feud with her father. The last thing they needed was a debate over Zeus and his unfair rules in regard to his many errant children. "We're running out of time, lass. We need to get ready and get to the temple." His brothers had surely arrived by now and the decree by Clotho to basically bed and wed Britt was fast approaching. He'd accomplished one and would have enjoyed a follow-up and another chance to get her with child, but Athena's timing sucked, as usual.

"So, it's true. You've found the tablets. Finally, now we can focus on finding the other females."

"Um, what other females?" Britt wrapped the bedding tighter around her body and scooted to the side of the bed.

Quinn watched her as she swung her legs over the edge and stood. Her hair loose around her shoulders, her glasses slightly askew, she'd never looked more beautiful.

Without a thought, he moved toward her, the need to finish what they'd begun so strong he'd almost forgot about his goddess mother watching his every move.

Ignoring Britt's question, Athena moved the owl to her shoulder. "She's not with child." Her mouth pinched, her tone accusatory. "So, not only have you broken the prophecy, she's not even pregnant. Your father managed to impregnate me with the six of you within moments."

Britt cleared her throat. "Um, I'm going to go get dressed." Shuffling, she made her way to her pile of clothes, dipped down, and scooped them up.

Quinn sighed again at the intrusion, his gaze locked on his mate's covered curves.

"I would have expected this from Trace, not you."

"And yet the world still spins, Mother. Once we meet up with Gavin, he'll perform the ceremony, we'll locate the tablet, and then everyone will leave so Britt and I can be alone." Quinn turned back toward Athena.

The goddess snorted, then a staff materialized in her right hand. "Lead the way."

Quinn held up a hand, "Nay. You've been gone for over a century, and then you show up now, looking for what exactly, Mother? Glory. Redemption? Did our father's disappearance once our training ended not prove to you his true intentions?"

Athena raised her staff and slammed it into the floor. The vibration ran through his body, stealing his breath.

"Please, you've been capable of surviving on your own since your tenth year. All of you. The sons I'm not able to claim should understand why I've kept my distance." Lightning flashed in her eyes. "You would have me break Zeus' decree I remain a virgin goddess in the eyes of man?" She widened her stance and held Quinn's gaze.

Banging sounded from the bedroom door.

"Quinn! Britt! Are you alright in there?" Mac's shout rang out.

A squeak traveled from the direction of the bathroom, and Britt stuck her head out. "Everything okay?"

Quinn rolled his eyes and turned his back on one of the most powerful beings in Olympus, and searched for the rest of his things. "We are not your blind followers, yet we would have appreciated more frequent check-ins." His mother was used to being followed, never questioned. Her followers had long ago vanished after the destruction of her temple at the acropolis, and she'd never gotten over it.

"Those damn Romans ruined everything. And don't get me started on the seventeenth-century Turks, the ingrates." Athena's voice rose with each word, till the mirror over the dresser cracked.

Shite. That's what he got for opening his mouth. He ignored her outburst and found his boots. The doorknob rattled, and Mac shouted, "Dammit, Quinn. Open the fucking door before I knock it down!"

The battling roars from his mother and brother triggered a piercing stab in his head. "Enough!" Quinn stomped to his door and flung it open. "Mac, she's your problem now." He waved his arm at their mother before spinning on his heels and marched to the bathroom.

"Mother?" Mac whispered. He bowed at the waist,

then ran straightened and ran a hand over his head. "What are you doing here?"

"Asked and unanswered," Quinn mumbled.

Britt emerged, dressed for their outing, her hair tamed into a long ponytail he instantly wanted to wrap his hand around, then use to bend her backward and capture her still swollen lips. Damn his family.

Turning away from his mate, Quinn addressed his brother. "Apparently, she sensed the breaking of the prophecy and decided to pop in." He ignored another snort from his mother. "The rest of the Brethren, they've arrived?"

"All but Trace. Still MIA. With luck, we won't need him." Mac's gaze stayed on their mother. "Will you be joining us at the temple?"

Athena looked from Britt to Quinn to Mac and back to Britt. "There's a chance to redeem yourselves in the eyes of the Fates. I understand Clotho gave you three days. You still have time to go through with the ceremony." She stepped closer to Quinn, raising her arm with her free hand open, waiting. "Time to get her with child, my son. It begins with you and..." Turning toward Britt, she nodded. Smiling, she offered her hand. " And you, Dr. Brittany Harmony."

Quinn watched as Britt took a hesitant step, then another, and raised an arm toward Athena. His lips curled up as she straightened her back, lifted her chin, and placed her hand in his mother's. Athena pulled Britt another step closer.

Unsure what his mother intended, Quinn rushed to

Britt's side and wrapped his arm around her waist, bracing for what came next.

Wind whipped throughout the room; an icy chill ran up his spine. He noticed Britt held perfectly still as his mother's eyes bored into hers. He'd never been prouder of another than he was in that moment.

"You are the key, and together you will now begin the destiny set forth for all the Brethren. Use your gift wisely and keep your grimoire close, my newest daughter." Athena's features softened as she gazed upon them. "And should your father make an appearance, tell him... tell him I have a surprise should he wish to visit."

Blinding white light filled the room and in a blink, his mother was gone. Britt slumped against him and laughed hysterically. They needed to leave. He scooped her up, cradling her close, and cursed at the timing of her breakdown. It'd been bound to happen. She'd been so strong up till this point, he'd begun to believe she was made of stone.

Striding through the house he met up with Mac outside. Mac was waiting for them, the SUV running and packed. "Is she alright?"

He nodded and with Mac's assistance placed her inside the vehicle.

Britt's laughter quieted. Quinn cradled her face, rubbing a thumb over her cheek. "Sweetheart, talk to me. Are you able to go through with this?"

Britt nodded, took in a deep breath, and let it out on a shaky sigh. Seconds crept by as uncertainty filled him. Was she strong enough after all she'd been through?

"Quinn, we need to leave. Now." Mac secured his seatbelt and caught his gaze in the rearview mirror.

"I know. Just one more minute." He noted the moon sinking into the horizon, dawn would be breaking soon. He buckled Britt in and did the same for himself before closing the door. He ran through his inventory and waited.

Britt sat up straighter then turned to him, a resolute expression on her beautiful face. "I'm so sorry, Quinn. Everything just hit me all at once."

At her words, he nodded at Mac, and they were off to the temple. To see if what was written in the scroll was true or yet another false lead.

Halfway to Chichén Itzá, Britt broke the silence with a soft chuckle. Concerned that she was losing it again, he grabbed her hand and held on tight. "It'll be fine, lass. We'll get through this together."

"It's not that. I've seen you in action. I'm not worried. Well, not much anyway."

"Tell me, what has you concerned?" Quinn lifted Britt's chin with his forefinger, checking her eyes. They were clear and bright. All signs of her previous hysteria were gone.

"Athena said the oddest thing right before she disappeared. She said, "keep your grimoire close.""

"Your spell book? Did you not bring it with you?"

"Not only did I not bring one, I've never had one."

TWENTY-EIGHT

Britt's statement hung in the air.

Quinn shrugged. "Perhaps you're meant to discover it once we are bound." He shifted to the edge of the seat and pointed toward a line of trees just beyond the entrance to the temple complex. "There, I sense our brothers. Mac, park next to that stand of trees.

She let the worry of finding her grimoire go, for now, as she drank in the magnificence of Chichén Itzá in the waning moonlight.

Britt scanned the area, catching three large men walking toward them in her peripheral vision. She recognized Roane, his shaved head hard to miss. Gavin followed, just as large and carrying a sword similar to Quinn's. The third brother was one of the two she'd yet to meet. He was by far the tallest of the group. Equally handsome as all the brethren, his brows were drawn together and lips pursed in a thin line as he looked from her to Quinn. Disapproval poured from him the closer he came to where they stood waiting.

Quinn clasped forearms with each brother, then returned to her side and placed his arm around her waist. "We have an hour. Britt, this grump over here is Keir. Good to see you brother, I didn't expect you'd make it."

"Alaska isn't as far as you often complain, Quinn."

Britt wondered at the tension she felt between the two, but there was little time to worry. She waited for Quinn to respond, but he ignored Keir.

"Roane, you and Gavin scout the opening and make entry. Myself, Mac, and Britt will enter from this side. Mac has already prepped you with Britt's ability to find objects, and we should know fairly quickly if one of the tablets is indeed inside. Once she pinpoints its location, Mac will alert you. Let's go." Quinn spun on his heel, not giving anyone a chance to argue.

Okay then. Quinn strode away without a backward glance. By the looks of the others, they were used to his "do as I say" commands. Gavin rolled his eyes, and Roane shook his head as they and Keir took off in the opposite direction.

Britt followed Quinn over the massive grounds. She held in her need to admonish his gruffness since they all, no doubt, were used to their eldest brother's ways.

The closer she came to the stone structure, the more she felt the instant draw. The step pyramid was what most of the world thought of when they heard the name Chichén Itzá. In reality, it was one of many structures in the large complex. It was also known as the Temple of Kukulcán and El Castillo, the castle.

"Quinn, hold up. You do know there is an archeological dig going on, right? And there are guards. No one can go in or out of the pyramid without the site director knowing and—"

"Settle, lass. We're not just anyone. Give me some credit," Quinn ground out between gritted teeth.

Wow. She'd hurt his feelings.

"I've got nothing on the infrared. The guard is probably on the other end of the complex. You pick up anything, Quinn?" Mac asked.

"No. All clear."

They were on the back side of the temple opposite the main entrance of the pyramid where the other three Brethren were headed. She was aware of only one entry into the temple at ground level, and it was too much of a risk to climb the steps, which would alert the guards to their presence.

Quinn and Mac seemed in no hurry to find an alternate way in, so she'd find it herself. A familiar itch began between her shoulder blades. Her desire to dig, to search, and discover overwhelmed her system.

Britt walked closer to the pyramid. She reached up and felt the rough edges and precise angles of one of the many thousands of stone blocks. She closed her eyes and absorbed the low vibration as it traveled throughout her system.

Something was inside.

Something wonderful.

Quinn came up behind her and pushed on three stones far above her head. A low rumble and scraping of stone broke the silence as a four-foot square section opened.

Stale air tickled her nose as she peered inside. "Nice trick. Is that one of your powers?"

"Nay. The Mayans built this as an escape route. Their enemies often attacked during religious ceremonies."

"And you know about that how?" Britt asked.

"Because I'm an old yet hot guy?"

She was shocked into silence by his humor and his devastating smile. Oh, no. She was in trouble. He was flirting with her.

Instead of answering him, she waited for him to enter the temple. She knew he expected a response, but she wasn't going to play. Her nerve endings were on overload from his unexpected smile and the treasure her senses screamed was inside.

Britt bent down to walk through the opening and bumped into his arm, blocking her from entering.

"What are you doing? I thought we came here to go inside?"

"Not yet. I'm using my Spidey senses. Need to make sure the bogeyman or more likely, a demon or two, isn't lying in wait for us."

Quinn stepped in front of her and placed her behind him. He stood still for so long, her frustration got the best of her, and she tried to sidestep him.

He barked out, "Wait."

She rolled her eyes and stuck out her tongue.

"I saw that."

"Of course you did."

"I can think of better uses for your tongue, lass. However, now's not the time."

She heard Mac snort. Damn, she forgot about him, but that didn't keep her from flipping him off without so much as a backward glance. Screw it. She pulled from Quinn's grasp and marched around him and toward the threshold of the opening.

Britt didn't get far. Quinn grabbed her from behind, picked her up, and swung her around. He loosened his grip, and her body slid down his until her ass was nestled up against his front—his very hard front.

"What you seem to keep forgetting, lass, is that I'm in charge. No one enters the temple until I give the all clear."

She looked down at his arm wrapped around her middle, and it struck her how much stronger he was than her. She hadn't allowed herself to accept that she was in any real danger of being hurt by him—until now. Ignoring the sexual chemistry they created, she wrapped her hands over his warm, muscular arm and tried to pry it away from her.

They may have slept together, but she wasn't going to let him dictate her movements. What she wouldn't give to have her promised powers now. She counted to ten, let out a deep breath through gritted teeth, and spoke as calmly as she could. "So, is it safe to enter, or do we have to wait for some kind of mystical sign before going in?"

She felt him come closer behind her. She held back a moan. This was turning into pure torture. She tried not to move. Any more friction would cause her to cry out with want. Why hadn't the unending need stopped once they'd had sex?

"Damn, Quinn. Could we get back on track here? You two will have plenty of time for hiding the salami after the ceremony."

Quinn released her at Mac's words. Turning Britt around to face him, he caught her chin in his hand. "We'll pick this up," his heated gazed burned her as he looked her up and down, "later."

Arrogant bastard. But she'd make him keep his promise, and then she'd somehow get him to take her back home.

"Sure, but then you promise to go back through the portal so I can get back to London where I belong. I won't tell a soul about you or the Brethren, or Athena, or any of this."

"How can you still fight the truth, lass? Must it always be one step forward, two steps back with you?"

He was right. What was wrong with her? She watched as he stomped off, picked up his bag and returned to the entrance. How was it possible to dislike him in one moment and want to get naked with him the next?

"I will lead. You stay behind me. No arguments. Mac, watch her as if your life depends on it. Because it does. What I say goes."

He pointed at her. "You agree, or you stay in the SUV. Understood?"

This was what he must have been like back when they warred with legions of demons centuries ago. His lips had thinned, his jaw stubbornly set, and his body primed for anything. And it turned her on. Where had this new attraction for alpha men come from?

She knew he didn't mean it. There was no way they'd find whatever object was calling to her even now and she'd yet to enter the temple. But she was done with the ridiculous back and forth. "You lead. I'll follow." She held his gaze and blew out a slow breath.

"Somehow, I don't find that reassuring. There'll be no words spoken unless I give a sign. Both Mac and I are armed. If we encounter demons, you hide. If there's an exchange of gunfire, you hide. But most importantly, if we find anyone in there, I do all the talking."

She didn't dare speak again as the need to find whatever was calling to her began to consume her thoughts. Britt gave Quinn what he demanded.

She submitted.

TWENTY-NINE

Quinn held back a chuckle. Yeah, he wasn't buying her quick submission to his demands.

Britt was headstrong and, in any other circumstance, a capable and strong person. But he didn't want her acting before she thought things through. She'd become too important to him. Once they were bound to one another, he'd loosen up. Probably.

They wound their way through the tunnels for the next half hour without any sign from Britt that she'd picked up anything. Quinn glanced behind him, noticing her brow furrowed in frustration. He was ready to break the no-speaking rule when he sensed an electric snap in the air. It wasn't any of his brothers. He'd been tapped into their bioenergy as they progressed through the temple, so if they were in danger, he'd know.

No, something else was inside the pyramid. Something inhuman. Damn.

He continued, stepping over remnants of the restoration effort. Tools were scattered about, waiting for first light and the archeologists to begin another day.

Another pulse of energy enveloped him, rapidly followed by at least a dozen more. "Mac, you feel that?"

"Yeah. Heavy. I'm feeling emotions which aren't mine."

"Demons," Quinn growled out.

"I felt it too. And what do you mean, demons? Oh, my lord, please tell me they're not all able to project images into our heads?" Britt scanned the area behind her, then looked at Quinn.

Quinn turned back to find her frozen in place. Worry lines had appeared at the corners of her mouth. Her breath came in shallow bursts. His dragon roared to life, pissed it couldn't shift and protect their mate.

Shite, he didn't have time to deal with an enraged dragon at the moment and pushed back on the beast's instincts, promising a flight soon.

Returning his attention to Britt, he held back a curse at the fear in her gaze. Fucking damn Dante. He'd give anything to wipe her encounter with the demon from her memory.

"Lass, take a deep breath. I willna let anything happen to you."

"He's here," she whispered.

"Nay. It's residual energy." The lie came easy—anything to wipe the worry off her beautiful face.

"How can you be so sure?"

The doubt in her voice struck him hard. "Trust me.

That's all I ask." Hundreds of years of being in charge of the Brethren hadn't prepared him for a scientist who defied him at every opportunity. He wanted, nay needed, to protect her from the monsters both above and below ground. He needed her to know she could count on him. Always.

She held his gaze and nodded. "Okay, but Quinn?"

"Yes, *mo chridhe*?" He lowered his voice, cupped her face, and feathered his thumb over her lower lip—his need for her rose to match his protective instincts. Quinn sighed and dropped his hand, and took in a cleansing breath. Now was not the time for seduction. He prayed once they were bound, the constant need for her would not override his ability to keep her safe.

"I'm feeling a different type of energy up ahead. It's definitely not residual. It's the rush of emotion plus an electric tingle I feel when I'm close to a special artifact. Often ancient. And it's never failed me. I can't explain it, nor am I able to bring it forth on a whim. It's stronger now than the sensation I briefly felt before we entered. And if demons or Dante is here... well, we need to find it quickly."

"He's not going to get his hands on you, Britt. I *willna* let that happen—ever." The emotion in his voice shook him. He would die for her, but he'd do his best to make sure today would not be that day.

Britt's shoulders visibly relaxed at his words. Her quick recovery pleased him.

"All right, if what you're feeling is stronger, hopefully, that means the object calling to you is close. Let's continue. Keir, Roane, and Gavin should meet up with us soon."

Quinn looked over her head and exchanged a look with Mac. His brother would protect Britt at any cost, so there was no need to say the words aloud. The nod he received confirmed the unspoken question.

They trekked deeper toward the center of the temple, where the air carried ghosts of priests and worshipers long buried. If one breathed deeply, the smell of incense lingered, and faint chanting still rang.

"Quinn?"

"What is it, lass?"

"It's here." Britt ran her hands over the walls. "We need to look for unnatural lines, anything that seems out of place. I don't think we'll find it in a chamber. Whatever it is, is hidden in the walls."

"Do you have any idea of what it may be? Are you able to tell the difference between, say, a religious object and a tablet?" Mac, still bringing up the rear, asked the question while keeping watch behind them.

"Typically? No. But this feeling is beyond the norm for me. On top of the tingling, I'm also experiencing an itch between my shoulders, one I can't quite reach. Not sure if that's because I know there's something dangerous lurking in the shadows or that this object is older than anything else I've ever found."

Quinn felt the dark presence she was describing. Something very dark had entered the temple, and it was coming closer. "I *dinna* think we have much more time.

Tell us, what do we need to do? Start digging or chipping away at the stone?"

"Are you kidding? No. Just no. There are rules to be followed. Protocols. We need to let the team leader know. There's no way we can—"

"There's no time. You feel something, right? Then we find what it is. Now."

"What's coming, Quinn? And don't think I don't notice every time you and Mac share that 'look.' I can handle whatever it is."

"We *dinna*—" A sonic boom interrupted Quinn's protest. The earth beneath their feet moved. Pebbles tumbled from the ceiling. He caught Britt as she swayed, steadied her, and covered her head just as a large chunk of stone rained down inches from her.

"Oh my god. Is it an earthquake?"

"No. Worse." Quinn held her tight, not willing to let her go yet.

"What's worse than an earthquake?" Britt's voice cracked.

"A pissed-off demon."

"Britt, I need you to figure out where we need to start. Once we locate the object, we need to get out of here."

"Dammit, we can't just start digging. It goes against everything I've been taught and stand for. I don't have anything to excavate properly."

She was pissed and beautiful, and she'd once again put him in his place. And turned him on.

"There's no need to yell. What did you think was

going to happen? We'd just walk up to whatever it is you're sensing lying around? So, I will ask you again; please show us where you think the object is. If you don't, I'm done being reasonable."

Her chin jutted out at his demand, and she stuck her fisted hands onto her hips. Strands of her hair had come free framing her face, and her eyes flashed. She was magnificent. But they were running out of time.

"Just point, Britt. Mac and I will do the rest."

Britt leaned against the temple wall and wiped beads of sweat from her brow. "If I do this, you owe me."

"Nay. I understand what we need to do goes against everything you've been taught about preserving digs, but we don't have that kind of time. Lass, this could be what we've been searching for. And since no one's found it yet, that has to mean something. That you're the one to have located it."

▲ ▲ ▲

WHY'D he have to pick now to be logical? Britt's gut churned. Nausea rose up as a further sign that she was onto something. The decision to go against her training as an archeologist hurt her heart, yet...it was as he said. Now or never.

"All right. But don't think I won't expect a favor for this." Her attempt at levity fell flat so she raised her arm and pointed to a spot just over his right shoulder. Her heart rate increased as she moved closer. She brushed past Quinn and placed a hand on the wall. The area on the wall was an innocuous location no one would suspect held an item of great worth.

A pounding emitted from the stone almost as fast as her pulse. She worked her fingers around it, noticing its warmth. She exposed its edges. "Here. It's about twelve inches square."

"Do you know how deep it goes?"

She closed her eyes and listened. "Maybe ten inches, give or take a fraction."

"That's pretty damn specific," Mac said.

Britt opened her eyes and smiled. She continued to stare at the stone, both hands now framing the spot where something was calling to her. "It's my gift," she whispered.

Another boom sounded. Not as loud as the first. They all stilled, waiting for an attack. Precious seconds ticked by; seconds she knew they were wasting. Britt moved back. "Now. Do it before I change my mind."

Before she finished speaking, Quinn punched a hole through the stone, then and another. She looked at his hands, knuckles barely bruised.

Her nausea subsided, and the hum in her veins settled into a steady rhythm.

Quinn reached into the small space and brought out a leather pouch the size of a grapefruit. Not a tablet. Her disappointment was instant. She hadn't realized how much she wanted the object to be one of the Emerald Tablets.

"We need to leave—now." Quinn pounded his fist on the wall.

"No, there's got to be more—" She doubled over in pain. The queasiness had returned full force. But why? They'd found an object. In the past, once she discovered an artifact, all of her symptoms vanished.

"Lass, what's wrong?" Quinn grasped her shoulders, keeping her from falling over.

Britt closed her eyes, tapping into her intuition. "Could you look again? I think there might be something else."

With one hand on her shoulder steadying her, Quinn reached back in.

"There's nothing but stone, Britt."

Beads of sweat formed on her face and the back of her neck burned. "Then punch another hole. Please." There had to be another object. She was on the verge of passing out.

Quinn did as she asked. On the third try, he broke through into another chamber. Britt blessedly felt relief from the pain in the same instant.

As dust settled, Quinn whispered, "Fuck me."

CHAPTER
THIRTY

Britt straightened as Quinn pulled a large object wrapped in decaying linen from the hole. She smoothed the wrinkled covering, exposing a corner. Emerald-green light bounced off the stone walls.

"My god, the power," she whispered. Her entire body hummed from the connection.

Another pulse of energy enveloped the tunnel and hung in the air. Time was running out.

"We need to protect her, Quinn. I know I'm not Gavin, but I can recite the words just as well." Mac dug through his backpack and produced a short rope. "I think you need to bind yourselves. Now. Otherwise, if he takes her, finding her will be next to impossible, even with your telepathic connection."

Quinn barked out a curse. "Mac's right, lass."

"Could you two stop talking as if I'm not here, please. Can't you use that thing you did back at the hotel and buy us time?" Britt tucked the treasure against her chest.

Quinn shook his head, and her stomach dropped.

"Lass, I hoped our binding to occur under better circumstances, but there's only one option available to us. I wanted to give you more time…"

"No, not like this." Britt felt a ball of hysteria form in the back of her throat. She was on the brink of losing her shit in spite of the otherworldly power she held in her hands.

"It's Dante. Somehow…damn it, he's managed to travel from his prison in hell." Quinn locked his gaze in the direction a new gust of putrid wind had emitted.

"You promised it wasn't him," Britt's voice trembled.

Quinn closed his eyes. "I know. I wanted to protect you." He turned to Mac. "I'm sensing he's not using technology. He's somewhere in the temple. And with him, thirty, maybe forty of his army. My sword…" A deep growl burst from his chest. "It's in the truck. Without it, I'm not sure we'll make it out of here."

"You mean with the tablet?" Britt asked.

"With our lives." Quinn's tone grim. He gathered her in his arms. "Forgive me." He whispered against her temple.

"Thank you, Dr. Harmony. I'll take that off your hands." A disembodied voice bounced off the stone walls.

"Dante," he growled.

Britt's body jolted.

Quinn turned her to his side, keeping her close. Britt

leaned into his muscular form and found instant courage for what was coming. Taking in a deep breath to calm her nerves, she sighed at his scent. Even in the dusty temple, he smelled of the sea.

"Perhaps this will persuade you." The Duke of Hell stepped out of the shadows of the junction formed by the connecting tunnel thirty yards away and held out his hand. A short, bald creature with skinny arms and leathery skin appeared. It handed him a black, square device.

"Technology has made things easier, but it's definitely taken some of the fun out of our hunting." Dante waved off the smaller, meek demon and tapped several times on the glass, then turned the screen toward them.

Even from so far away, Britt was able to make out a young woman's face, bloody and bruised. Her head had fallen forward. A large hand appeared and yanked the woman's head up. She let out a string of curses.

"*Tsk. Tsk.* So unladylike." Dante directed to the poor woman filling the screen.

Britt's stomach sank as she realized the woman reacted to Dante's words.

"She can hear us?" Britt accused.

Dante grinned. "Of course. And see us. I wanted to make sure there's no confusion about who's in my custody. I'm sure you'd prefer to have this family reunion in person, but this is the best I could do on short notice."

Quinn put his body in front of Britt. "What

happened to being tethered to hell? Or is this another one of your tricks?"

"No trick. All treat. For me, that is. Lucifer gave me a hall pass. Or, maybe...not." Dante chuckled. "He's desperate these days. Let's just say I merely exploited a loophole and here I am."

Britt shivered at Dante's words. She braced herself against the highlander's broad back. She noted the demon was no longer the handsome man he'd projected himself to be just a day ago. His smile, pure evil. Grotesque. His black hair slicked back, showcasing twin onyx horns curled low against his skull.

"Do you know this woman, Quinn?" Britt asked, confused over the woman's identity but no less horrified for her. Nausea erupted over the treatment she'd suffered.

Quinn shook his head. "No. You're sure she's not someone you could be related to?"

Britt frowned. "No. She has green eyes, but that's where the similarity ends. I'm positive I've never seen her before."

Dante growled. "I find it hard to believe you don't recognize your own blood, Dr. Harmony."

"I know everyone that is related to me, asshole. And none are living." Britt held her ground, "I'm the last one."

Dante smirked and turned the screen back toward himself.

"You hear that, Sierra? Britt doesn't recognize her own cousin. Such a shame the family has grown apart.

Good thing I found you. Now you both can enjoy a long-overdue reunion."

"Dante, what in the hell are you playing? Britt just told you she has no family." Quinn widened his stance. "Mac, get the others here, now."

"There almost here." Mac stepped closer to Britt and whispered, "Don't take your hand off Quinn. The demon is going to try and compel you away. As long as you two are touching that can't happen."

Dante took a step closer. "You see, my love, my only goal is to bring you and your family together. Only I can do that for you. And of course, give you everything he can't."

As Mac had predicted, Britt's body shook at the compulsion she heard in Dante's voice. Shaking off the creepy-crawly sensation, she shifted the tablet and tucked it under her right arm, and looped her left through Quinn's.

Dante let loose a crazed laugh. "What can this shifter do? Give you an old castle to call home. Fly you around on his back, and impregnate you to pass on his sire's alien blood in the hopes of saving the weak-willed humans?" The whites of the demon's eyes flashed blood red.

"Ah, Britt, I can give so much more. Come with me, fulfill your destiny with me, and you have my word I'll find the rest of your poor lost cousins."

Cousins? No, she had no one. Dante had to be lying... but what if he wasn't? Britt swayed. Dante's voice echoed in her mind. *Six of you. All mine. Step forward, my love, and they will be safe.*

"Britt, fight him. Use your gift, your magic." Urgency laced Quinn's words. "Tap into the tablet, *mo chridhe.*"

Quinn's plea made no sense. She had no magic. But she had plenty of rage.

Pent-up rage at being taken from her life.

Rage at the demon for taking another woman and using her as a bargaining chip.

And rage toward her father for keeping the truth from her.

All this time she could have been preparing herself to stand up against a demon bent on owning her. Standing and fighting alongside the man to who Fate decreed she belonged. Pounding footfalls rang out the chamber as Roane, Gavin and Keir raced in, their shouts filling her ears. "You need to bind yourselves, now." And "I'll perform the ceremony."

Five towering brethren surrounded her. Britt pushed aside her rage, but grief quickly filled its space. "Why should I believe you? My father never spoke about any cousins. He had no brothers. No sisters. We were alone in the world," Britt shouted.

She'd never let despair overtake her, and she wasn't going to let Dante have her or the woman he claimed to be her cousin. She pushed against Quinn. A craving to destroy the demon began to well up within her. Unlike her response to the emerald tablet, this was sharper. The hair on her body rose, static electricity swirled around her.

Quinn looked over his shoulder at his brothers. "Protect her." Drawing out his dagger, he pushed Britt behind him. "Hold onto my belt loop, mate. We need to maintain physical contact."

Dismissing her as if she'd instantly obey him, well, she'd let him believe that.

Quinn addressed Dante, "This will be the last time you're in her presence, demon."

The rest of the brethren drew closer. Someone placed a hand on her shoulder. Gavin. He began chanting. Ancient Gaelic. She looked up to see Gavin grasping Quinn's shoulder as well.

Dante spared a glance at Quinn, then continued, "So, yet another secret your father kept from you. Britt, I am sorry you had to grow up without him, truly. His death was tragic, but it was the only way to put you on the right path. To me."

Britt let out a howl. "It was you that day? You bastard."

"Yes." Dante grinned, tossed the device aside, and took another step forward. "Tell your brother to shut up, Quinn. This is your last chance, Britt. Or Sierra dies."

"No!" Quinn roared and tossed the dagger.

THIRTY-ONE

"Looks as if you found her, son."

Britt jolted at the new voice. Quinn wrapped an arm around her waist, pulling her in tight. She felt his body vibrate and his breathing quicken. "Quinn, are you alright?" She looked up at his face, realizing he'd frozen, his gaze narrowed on the man who magically appeared.

Just when she thought her life couldn't get weirder, the universe laughed and said, *"Hold my beer."*

Grumblings from the rest of the Brethren grew loud behind them.

"Lass, I'd like you to meet my father, Tiegh."

Tiegh stood a few yards away, at least a foot taller than Quinn. He had light-green skin but otherwise looked human. He bowed toward her. "I see you have your hands full, my dear." Tiegh flashed Britt a smile. "By all means, carry on. I had no idea there'd be so many in attendance at the discovery of my missing tablet."

A frustrated growl emitted from the demon. "What is this? Bringing daddy into our...disagreement, Quinn. How unlike you." Removing the knife from his chest as if it were a mere nuisance and letting it fall to the ground, Dante sneered, turning toward Tiegh. "I suggest keeping your otherworldly abilities out of this. After all, you wouldn't want to risk losing any more mates."

Tiegh's expression turned stormy at Dante's declaration. "Explain, demon."

Dante smirked. "Oh, I'll leave that for Britt to share. She could have ensured the girl's safety, but her ignorance comes at a great cost." Dante's red eyes briefly dimmed. He turned his attention from Britt back to Tiegh. "You're too late, Thoth. I have one of the fated mates. Wonder who she's destined for? No matter, without her you won't be able to fulfill the Fate's prophecy now, will you? Too bad, really. I was hoping for more of a challenge, but Sierra was so easy to find. Maybe the next one will prove more difficult."

Tiegh raised a hand toward Dante. Quinn shouted a warning, "Not here. You're power's too great. You'll bring the temple down around us all. Meet us at the castle. We have this under control."

His father leveled Quinn a look that could melt the stone around them. "You risk much, Quinn. I take orders from no one."

A loud cough of "No shit" came from the direction of his brothers.

"Fine. Stay. But if you interfere, I swear the demon race will be the last of your worries."

Britt ignored the chest-pounding going on between father and son. Her skin's itching had increased, and it was becoming uncomfortable. It had begun after she brushed her fingers over the cool emerald tablet.

"Ah well, that's too bad. I would have liked to see what daddy's capable of. So, I'll just take my leave. But know this, the mates your Brethren were promised, I will find them all before you figure out where the next woman lives."

"Tough talk from a mere Duke of Hell. My bets are on the rest of my brothers finding their mates before you. And we will find Sierra. That's a promise. I suggest you go back to that prison you crawled out from, Dante. Once the next generation is born, your false hope to take over humankind will be but a distant wet dream." Quinn's dragon stirred; it wanted out—wanted a piece of the demon.

"You may have won this battle. Found the first tablet and bound Britt to you. But do you think I'd be so foolish as to show you everything I'm capable of? Know this, when you think you've found the next mate, I'll already have her."

"Wait, Quinn. We need to do something to get him to give up Sierra's location. I feel like... I need to...hurt him. My palms are on fire. Please, let me try?" Britt spread her legs, pushing all her strength through them, anchoring her to the ground. A flow of energy traveled through her body, settling between her breasts before snapping and spreading along her arms, then pooled into her palms as the itching intensified. Her head pounded to the beat of her heart. *What's happening to me?*

Quinn tore his gaze from Dante and turned around. "Your eyes, lass. They're glowing." He stepped aside, giving her a clear line of sight to Dante. "It's your power, *mo chridhe*. Our binding has set it free."

His tone and words bolstered her confidence. Whatever was happening to her, she knew deep down she could handle it. It urged her to attack the demon, but before she did, she addressed Quinn. "One of these days, you're going to tell me what that means, husband."

Britt raised her arms toward Dante. The itching had stopped. In its place, warmth infused her arms, hands, and palms. Something awesome was about to happen, and she felt practically giddy at the power flowing through her.

The demon began to laugh. "Oh, Britt. It's such a pity you chose poorly. You would have made the perfect duchess to sit by my side. No matter, your cousin will do." His form flickered in and out.

"No!"

▲▲▲

QUINN WATCHED as his mate threw all her weight forward and pushed her newfound power through her palms toward Dante. A ball of white fire shot from her fingertips toward the demon, enveloping his entire form. Arms engulfed in flames, he flailed about. The demon let out an unholy scream, moved forward two steps, then stopped.

Dante's head and body shook so violently as the demon fought the flames, Quinn thought he would explode. Maniacal laughter erupted from the demon as his body burned. Two of his soldiers, plus the deformed creature from earlier, appeared and began beating back the flames.

"Nice trick, witch," Dante howled as he crawled to his knees, pushing himself into a wobbly stance. "But I'm a Duke of Hell. You think this will keep me down for long? You will be mine, Britt. And then you will beg me for mercy." He bellowed the evil promise before falling to his knees.

Quinn turned his focus on Britt in time to see her wincing as skin melted off the demon's face and hands. Collapsing to the dirt-packed floor of the temple, Dante wailed, "Brigid, your progeny will be mine!"

Dante was dragged away, disappearing into shadows.

Quinn turned to his brothers. "Let's get the hell out of here."

"You don't have to tell me twice. Tablet's secured. I'm ready when you are." Mac swung a beat-up leather backpack up over his shoulder.

"What are we going to do about him?" Roane stepped to Quinn's side, pointing a thumb toward their father.

Tiegh, or whatever the hell he was going by now, remained silent, watching. Centuries had passed since any of them had been in the presence of their father. Mistrust and anger oozed from every pore of Quinn's being. Before he could request it of them, his brethren formed a half circle facing their sire, keeping Britt securely behind them.

The four brothers stood shoulder to shoulder, their alternate forms briefly flashing as a show of unity.

Quinn had no time to warn Britt before he heard her shocked gasp. He turned in time to watch her crumble to the ground.

THIRTY-TWO

"I'll take that." Tiegh reappeared next to Mac, reaching for the backpack and the tablet.

Quinn's head whipped around in time to see Mac spinning away from their sire. Could the five of them take him?

Britt stirred in his arms. Torn between keeping the tablet from his father and protecting his mate was a near-impossible choice, yet Britt was his life now and Quinn would choose her above all else.

What did Tiegh have planned with the sudden reappearance in their lives? None of them truly knew what their father was capable of beyond the small glimpses he'd shown them when he'd tasked them with reclaiming the Emerald Tablets.

She'd been unable to claim them as her own by Zeus' decree. He wanted her to remain the Virgin Goddess in the eyes of her devoted followers. Athena was forced to turn over their rearing to others as she trained them in secret.

On their twentieth birthday, she too disappeared from their lives. What the Brethren knew of both their parents barely filled a cup. And now in a matter of days they'd both reappeared. What was going on?

Mac's shout of "No!" filled the temple. Roane, Gavin, and Keir charged forward. It would take all the Brethren to prevent Tiegh from overpowering Mac. But they were one short. They needed Trace. Early in their training, Athena had warned that it would take all six of them combining their power to overtake Tiegh, should the need arise.

Their selfish baby brother's disappearing act was going to cost them dearly.

"Go," Britt whispered. "I'm fine."

Quinn helped her stand, placed a too-brief kiss on his mate's lips, and rejoined his brothers. Their father's eyes widened. Quinn wasn't sure if it was pride or shock flashing in Tiegh's gaze as they stood against him.

"I understand your concern, my sons. However, things have changed since I gave you the responsibility of recovering the tablets. Man's perversion has grown. They teeter on a ledge between redemption and outright demon corruption. Neither is a foregone conclusion; however, I fear Lucifer's infiltration of the human world will soon become too much to defeat."

Quinn took a step forward, keeping Britt securely behind him. "We've barely begun. What makes you believe we won't succeed?"

Tiegh's eyes narrowed, his gaze roamed from one brother to the next. "When the real prophecy is fulfilled, and only then, will I fulfill my pact with the Fates."

Quinn bellowed in frustration. "Your pact? What do you mean? The prophecy says your progeny, along with our mates and our children, will defeat the demons. With the tablets." Quinn's dragon fought to emerge at the revelation that what he'd suspected of their destiny was coming to pass. Something vital had been held back.

"So, what is real and what is not, sire?" Gavin stepped forward. He'd had the added pressure of being tasked with performing the binding ceremony, without which, the destined matings could not occur.

Centuries of hiding to make certain he survived had created deep-seated trust issues Quinn wasn't sure Gavin could overcome.

"Have you not discovered? Any of you? The Fates are...fickle bitches." Tiegh's eyes blazed with hatred at the mention of the three females even the all-powerful Zeus couldn't strike down.

Tiegh avoided the question and blamed the Fates. Creating more questions and doubt that Quinn and his brothers could ever trust their father or anyone again.

"Tell us what we need to know. Why would you set us up to fail—" Quinn lost his balance as the earth beneath his feet, and everyone else's, shifted. A loud roaring rumbled through the passageway.

"Challenge me now and the Fates will cut your lives short. Even yours, Quinn, even after discovering and binding yourself to Britt. Clotho's deadline approaches and your mate's not yet with child. If I were you, and in a sense, I once was when I made my pact with Zeus and the Fates...just get your mate home. Now."

As his father spoke, Quinn thought he noticed a momentary vulnerability overtake his father, a slight softening in his face. Then, just as quickly, Tiegh's lips thinned, and a new determination filled his gaze.

"Stand down. All of you. Discover your mates, create the next generation, and fulfill the prophecy as you've been told. That part is true enough. Then and only then, will the Brethren be strong enough to banish Lucifer, his legions, and the corrupted humans who follow the fallen angel's path."

Quinn looked to Mac. His brother's stance hadn't changed. Rigid and taught, Mac's knuckles turning white as he gripped the backpack.

"I will have the tablet with or without your willingness." Tiegh touched Mac's shoulder, and both were gone. Vanished.

"The fuck!" Roane roared.

"Can we follow Mac's energy trail?" Keir raced to the empty spot Mac had occupied, his tone laced with disbelief.

Quinn strode over to Britt, bewilderment on her dust-covered face. "We need to leave now. The workers are on their way."

"Wait. Hold on just a damn minute. What the hell just happened? Your father appears, disappears. And your brothers...they shifted, but they weren't like you...

what were those creatures?" Britt sucked in a deep breath, her shoulders dropping in defeat.

Quinn looked over to see Roane, Gavin and Keir arguing over whether to stay longer, believing Mac would be returned. It wasn't likely. Their father could have easily retrieved the tablet with or without Mac.

"Enough. We carry on and get my mate to safety." Quinn would then be able to finally breathe deeply once she was back in the castle. Tiegh obviously wanted Mac for a reason and they'd figure it out after returning to Scotland.

Confident his brother could handle himself, Quinn grabbed and squeezed Britt's hand. "Ah, lass. I never said we're all dragon-shifters."

Tugging her close, and ignoring more questions, they raced through the temple's hidden exit, Quinn sealing it behind them. They made it to the SUV just as a pair of guards entered the complex's grounds.

Breaking hard near the portal, Quinn calculated how much time remained. The first tablet was once again safe, and Dante was down and out—for now—and Quinn had his mate. He now only had the decree from Clotho and Tiegh to worry about.

Stepping through the swirling purple-and-blue vortex, they arrived just as early-evening shadows criss-crossed the Scottish countryside. Quinn cradled Britt tight to his chest, capturing her lips in a soul-crushing kiss. He'd give her the words once he had her home—without an audience. He owed her for the rush of the binding ceremony.

Quinn ordered his still-arguing brothers to stay clear of the castle for a few hours, then shifted into his dragon form and flew his mate home.

⬥⬥⬥

CLIMBING the stairs to his room, their room, Quinn felt the deadline crushing down on him. Being ordered to get busy by one of the Fates wasn't the best way to begin their marriage, but the need to bury himself deep and plant his seed within his mate had nothing to do with Clotho, and everything to do with ensuring Britt was his —forever.

Britt tugged on his arm, bringing them both to a halt on the landing. "Is this really happening, Quinn? I mean this isn't some weird dream, right? We found one of the Emerald Tablets, got married, well...bound, your father shows up, takes it *and* Mac, and now I'm a full-fledged goddess, or witch who just fried a demon, and oh, your brothers. What are they?"

Quinn took her beautiful face in his hands. "You're not at full power—yet. We need to figure out how to find your grimoire. And as for the Brethren, we were each given an alternate form by Athena at birth. A dragon for me, Keir's a wolf, Roane's a grizzly, Gavin's a well, he's a bit of an anomaly. He's yet to shift, and Mac's a panther."

He watched as Britt took it all in, her eyes wide but

no hint of fear to be seen. She'd come to accept him as a dragon, so why not his brothers' shifter forms.

"Wait, that's five. What about Trace. The missing brother?"

"Trace is a Phoenix." Quinn gathered her hands in his, waiting for more questions.

Britt frowned. "Okay. I'm sure I'll eventually keep them straight. So, you think I'll need a grimoire?"

His head buzzed at the abrupt subject change. "I would expect so, since until today, you've never wielded magic, just used it to find objects. Don't worry, lass. We'll figure it out together."

"Huh, I guess that makes sense, my own book of spells." Her frown bloomed into a wide smile. "Anyway, don't we have something else left to do?"

Quinn's heart swelled. That's what he loved about Britt. Not only was she smart, beautiful, and sexy as hell, but she was resilient. One of the strongest women he'd ever met. "Yes, we do, but first I need to know that you're not upset with me. About the binding ceremony, I mean." *Tell her you idiot. Tell her you love her.*

"No, no it was the right thing to do. I wanted to go through with it. I wish... I just wish my father could have been here to see that the little goddess-witch had found her highlander prince." Britt's eyes filled with unshed tears.

"Nay, love. A dragon-shifter. I'm no prince."

"Love? You love me, even though it's been less than a week since we met?" A single tear streamed down her cheek.

Quinn brushed it away. "Aye, you captured my heart on that first day, lass. First, when you boldly opened the door and fell out of a moving vehicle—"

"And second?" she whispered.

"Every moment afterward."

"Dammit, Quinn you're going to make me cry." She laughed and wiped both eyes. "Well, I guess I'm doing that already."

"How about you kiss me instead, *mo chridhe*?"

"Deal." Britt pressed her body against his, winding her arms around his neck and kissed him lightly before pulling back. "I love you, my dragon prince."

Quinn growled at the chaste kiss, but his heart pounded until he thought it'd escape its cage. He hadn't realized how badly he needed to hear those words until just this moment. He scooped his mate into his arms and laughed as she squealed.

He strode into the bedroom and all thoughts of prophecy faded as he undressed them. Britt's bold gaze increased his need to touch, to consume her. He read a matching desire in her eyes as he walked her backward to the bed, gently pushed her down, covering her body with his.

Dipping his head, he kissed her until they broke apart gasping for air. "That was the kiss I needed."

Britt wrapped her legs around his waist, pressing her heat into his aching cock. Quinn groaned then took himself in hand and entered his mate. He slowly filled her, pulled back and repeated the torturous glide between her folds, over and over.

"Quinn, I need you," Britt murmured silkily as her inner walls clamped down on his cock.

"You have me," Quinn ground out, wanting this moment to last.

"No, I mean now." She lifted her hips, letting out small moans as she rode him, urging him to match her speed.

"Always with the demands." He grinned. Quinn increased his tempo, thrusting into her. The sounds of their lovemaking and her pleasure filled his ears. He reached between their slick bodies, teasing her hard bud as he pounded into her, bringing them both to the very edge. Britt screamed his name, her orgasm triggering his own.

Minutes later—or maybe an hour—it was hard to tell as time ceased to matter, Quinn pulled from her warmth, gathering her close. Spooning behind her, he spread a palm over her belly. She covered his hand with her own and sighed.

Quieting his thoughts, he listened, completely in tune with his mate. A tingle then a sharp spark enveloped and warmed his hand.

"Quinn? Is that?"

He brushed his lips against her temple. "It is, my love."

The next generation had begun.

EPILOGUE

Britt reached across the bed in search of her husband. Her eyes popped open when she found the bed empty. Quinn's pillow was still warm, so he couldn't be far. She stretched her limbs and replayed the night's events. Her skin, still flushed from the last round of lovemaking.

She felt loved and couldn't wait for his return. Placing her hands on her abdomen, she replayed the unbelievable moment she felt their child quicken in her womb. Was it her magic? Or perhaps Quinn's alien DNA combined with a Greek goddess' that made it possible?

Oh, my God. Athena would be her child's grandmother. Would she now involve herself in their lives? More importantly, would Tiegh?

Britt's thoughts drifted away from the world's most unlikely grandparents to her dreams from last night. She'd dreamt of her childhood and her father's fairy tales. In his way, he'd been educating her; faulting him now was useless. She'd do her best to keep his memory alive through her son.

Yes, a son. Her's and Quinn's. Nestled deep within her womb.

How she knew she carried a son was as simple as taking her next breath. She just knew.

Her mind wandered, words drifted, unattached. As she attempted to make sense of them, she sat upright in bed. Her heart raced at what instantly became clear. The spell, her spell. The one she was to use—to bring forth her grimoire.

Closing her eyes, she began chanting. A warm wind entered the room, swirled around her and lifted, then tangled her hair about her shoulders. She held out her hands, palms up. Her body bowed—a jolt of energy traveled through her. She repeated the words for a second time. The speed of the wind increased. She opened her eyes and spoke the words a third and final time.

"Goddess, witch, my destiny begun,

Send thy tome of bountiful spells,

As I ask, so mote it be."

With the final word ringing in her ears, she looked down to discover a leather-bound book in her lap. The cover was embossed with a shimmering gold Celtic knot in the center of the triple goddess symbol. She ran her hands reverently over the raised emblems.

A flash of a woman's eyes, similar in color to hers, filled her head. Were they Sierra's or perhaps another mate yet to be discovered.? Eager to share everything with Quinn, she tossed back the bedsheets.

In the doorway stood her husband, a look of wonder on his face.

"Words I didn't know were inside me... oh, my, they were there, waiting for me to unravel, to make order of them all. Oh, and the stories I had buried in grief when my father died. And now—"

Quinn joined her in bed and wrapped his arms around her. "I heard. Now what, my gorgeous goddess, my witch?"

Pounding on the door filled the room. "Quinn, I must speak with you." Mac's hoarse voice rang out.

Quinn froze at the sound of his brother's voice.

Mac had returned!

"Britt, I—"

"Go. He needs you."

Quinn crushed her mouth under his. Britt melted at his touch, her need for him great. But his brother also needed him, and they now had forever. She firmly pushed Quinn back. "Go see what happened. I'm just glad he's safe."

"Exactly, he's safe. What could be so important that he chances interrupting our honeymoon?" Quinn left their bed and stormed over to the door, flinging it open. "This had better be good, Mac. Did you not sense the others are not present within the castle?" Quinn bellowed.

Chuckling, Britt burrowed back under the down comforter as she listened to their fading voices arguing while they retreated down the hallway. His brethren were now her family. She looked forward to helping them search for their mates. Then there was their alternate forms—incredible. The initial shock she'd felt had melted into, well, awe. And she couldn't help but think of her father. He would have loved meeting real-life shifters, and his grandchild.

Her path had never been clearer than in this moment. Their child, would be the first of many. For them and for the other Brethren.

Britt would use her unveiled power against Lucifer and Dante, for he would unfortunately and eventually recover. And now, with the knowledge she held in her hands, she'd learn then instruct the rest of the Brethren's mates—guiding them through their journey —their shared destiny.

Britt cracked open the centuries-old leather. "Now the real adventure begins."

▲ ▲ ▲

Thank you for reading Britt and Quinn's story. If you have a moment, I hope you consider leaving a review.

What to read next?
WOLF'S MATE is Keir's book

FATED TO THE PHOENIX is Trace's book

Brethren's Castle - Scotland Highlands

Also by Debra Elise

TANGLING SERIES

THE IDAHO OUTLAWS SERIES

RESCUED BY LOVE: LATER IN LIFE

MOUNTAIN MEN OF PINEVILLE SERIES

PINEVILLE FIRE & RESCUE SERIES

PINEVILLE PROTECTORS SERIES

STAND ALONE STORIES

PARANORMAL FANTASY SERIES

THE BRETHREN'S LEGACY

ABOUT THE AUTHOR

Debra Elise, a *USA Today* Bestselling Author, writes steamy contemporary and paranormal romance. She lives with her younger trophy husband in the beautiful Pacific Northwest. They also have two young adult sons who have promised to never read her stories.

A self-proclaimed extroverted introvert, when not writing or procrastinating, she enjoys a strong cup of coffee and a good nap.

Visit Debra at www.debraelise.com